Bail

Bailey Bradford has created another impressive addition to this series which is best read in sequence. I especially enjoyed the mystery regarding the powerful wolf shifter. ~ *Literary Nymphs*

I really liked Paul and Justice's story. Because of what Paul suffered, the pace of parts of the story were slower and portrayed very gently with a lot of sweetness. I enjoy this series very much and am thankful that Bailey Bradford indulges my need for shifters and men loving on men! ~ *Rainbow Book Reviews*

This story has three of my favorite things: shifters: check. Hot man on man sex: check. Felines: check, check and check. I loved this book; Paul and Justice are great together. Justice helps Paul heal in a way that Paul never expected him to. You can see Paul use his fury to his advantage and fight against the fear and fight back against his attackers. I'm definitely going to follow this series. ~ *Mrs Condit Reads Books*

Totally Bound Publishing books by Bailey Bradford:

Southwestern Shifters
Rescued
Relentless
Reckless
Rendered
Resilience
Reverence
Revolution
Revenge

Southern Spirits
A Subtle Breeze
When the Dead Speak
All of the Voices
Wait Until Dawn
Aftermath
What Remains
Ascension
Whirlwind

Love in Xxchange
Rory's Last Chance
Miles to Go
Bend
What Matters Most
Ex's and O's
A Bit of Me
A Bit of You
In My Arms Tonight
Where There's A Will

Leopard's Spots
Levi
Oscar
Timothy
Isaiah
Gilbert

Esau
Sullivan
Wesley
Nischal

Mossy Glenn Ranch
Chaps and Hope
Ropes and Dreams
Saddles and Memories

Yes, Forever
Yes, Forever: Part One
Yes, Forever: Part Two
Yes, Forever: Part Three
Yes, Forever: Part Four
Yes, Forever: Part Five

Breaking the Devil

Leopard's Spots

JUSTICE

BAILEY BRADFORD

Justice
ISBN # 978-1-78184-670-4
©Copyright Bailey Bradford 2013
Cover Art by Posh Gosh ©Copyright September 2013
Interior text design by Claire Siemaszkiewicz
Totally Bound Publishing

This is a work of fiction. All characters, places and events are from the author's imagination and should not be confused with fact. Any resemblance to persons, living or dead, events or places is purely coincidental.

All rights reserved. No part of this publication may be reproduced in any material form, whether by printing, photocopying, scanning or otherwise without the written permission of the publisher, Totally Bound Publishing.

Applications should be addressed in the first instance, in writing, to Totally Bound Publishing. Unauthorised or restricted acts in relation to this publication may result in civil proceedings and/or criminal prosecution.

The author and illustrator have asserted their respective rights under the Copyright Designs and Patents Acts 1988 (as amended) to be identified as the author of this book and illustrator of the artwork.

Published in 2013 by Totally Bound Publishing, Newland House, The Point, Weaver Road, Lincoln, LN6 3QN, United Kingdom.

No part of this book may be reproduced, scanned, or distributed in any printed or electronic form without permission. Please do not participate in or encourage piracy of copyrighted materials in violation of the authors' rights. Purchase only authorised copies.

Totally Bound Publishing is an imprint of Total-E-Ntwined Limited.

If you purchased this book without a cover you should be aware that this book is stolen property. It was reported as "unsold and destroyed" to the publisher and neither the author nor the publisher has received any payment for this "stripped book".

JUSTICE

Dedication

We are all so much stronger than we think. Hold on, love each other, be kind and enjoy life.

Chapter One

The music sucked, but Paul Hardy didn't care. The music didn't matter any more than the bad lighting or the lack of attractive prospects. He wasn't picky. Just about any guy would do. As long as it wasn't a guy he'd already been with. Paul didn't do repeats.

It was for that reason he was at a different bar than the ones he'd been going to. Denver, Colorado had quite a few popular gay bars and clubs, but Paul wasn't bothering with places like that, where the good boys and girls went to play. He didn't want anything more than to get off, but even that was secondary to his true purpose, if he were to believe the shit his brother Preston had spewed at him earlier that evening.

Paul shoved all of that aside before he could get mad all over again. It had nothing to do with the fact that his brother might have been right. *He wasn't. I'm out to get laid because it fucking feels good, not because I think that's all I'm good for. Preston's so wrong. I'm not letting anyone fuck me. I'm the one taking control every time.*

A little niggling voice in his head pointed out that he'd always preferred to bottom, had liked his men growly and on the dominant side…before.

Then his mind balked at the 'before' part and Paul approached the closest guy in order to shut up his annoying conscience.

"Hey," the man muttered. He licked his lips as Paul looked him over.

Shorter even than Paul's five-and-a-half-feet height, too thin for it to be natural. The man's bones seemed too big for his scrawny frame, and there was a shady look about him. His eyes were too bright, too bloodshot. Paul shook his head. He didn't have many standards, true, but he wouldn't risk taking advantage of someone who was too fucked up to make a decision.

"Not hot enough for you?" the man snarked. "You aren't a prize either, ginger boy."

Paul raked him with a cold look and walked off. He hadn't come there to fight. His cheeks burned and he was glad of the crappy lighting. Used to be he'd bleached and dyed his hair, used fading creams and even makeup to try to hide his freckles.

Of course he could never hide all of the freckles—they were everywhere, sprinkled over his face, denser on his shoulders, then a little sparser down the rest of his body. He even had freckles on his dick and balls. Those were places he'd never hated the damned things enough to try bleaching them off.

It'd been a long time since he'd tried to hide his hair and change his complexion. Paul still hated being coloured in like a joke from God, but he didn't have the energy to fight it. Didn't have the money, either. His job at LuAnne's Bakery didn't pay all that much.

There was nothing wrong with his hair or his freckles, he knew that somewhere inside, but it'd sure made him a target more than once. Everyone seemed to be hating on people like him, and had been for a while. Paul had thought it'd have died down by now, all the ginger jokes, but no.

Add to that, his orange hair and freckles had made him a coveted prize on the human trafficking market. Once his true colouring had been uncovered, there'd been a bidding frenzy…

Paul repressed a shudder as he looked for someone, anyone, to distract him from his thoughts. There were certainly enough men in the place. He could hardly walk without brushing against someone else.

When anyone dared to grab at him, Paul snarled and smacked their hands aside. He didn't put on a friendly face, and he wasn't there to be manhandled. Just because he was short and on the thin side didn't mean he was a bottom looking for a big, strong man to fuck him into the wall. It didn't mean that at all.

Stereotypes—Paul hated them, even if, a couple of years before, he'd been one himself. He wasn't now, and people needed to get over thinking he was.

Paul shook off a hand clamping around his wrist, or tried to. He didn't even view the appendage as being attached to anyone, because he didn't give a shit who it belonged to, up until the point where he didn't easily free himself.

Then anger and fear pinged off his nerves like a pinball fired at warp speed. Paul glared up at the man holding onto him. The twisted smile and excitement in the stranger's eyes reminded Paul of all the things he was trying to forget.

His heart slammed hard a few times before racing. The shiver worked its way over Paul before he could stop it. He snapped his mouth shut, because gaping like an idiot wasn't going to help him any. No sign of weakness would. Paul had learnt there was only one language brutal people—brutal things—understood.

He slammed the palm of his other hand against the man's throat before even consciously thinking about it. Paul's survival instinct was immediately in high gear. The hand holding onto his wrist was gone in an instant.

"You fucking punk-ass bitch!" someone shouted at him. Paul didn't hang around to see who. He wasn't a coward, but he wasn't fucking stupid, either.

Running was impossible in the crowded place. He elbowed and shoved his way towards the front doors, aware that he was being chased. If the guy he'd hit had friends, Paul would end up getting the shit beat out of him—at the very least—should they catch him.

But once he hit the doors, he could lose them. Being short had its good qualities, and one of them was that he had speed taller men lacked most of the time.

As long as they're humans. If they were shifters...Paul thrust the door open and hit the pavement running. The bouncer yelled at him, but Paul just kept going. It wasn't like he'd done anything wrong, except maybe, possibly seriously injure a man.

Shit! Had he hit the guy hard enough to kill him? Paul just didn't know. His emotions were nonexistent unless his brother goaded him into an argument or he felt threatened, at which point he tended to overreact.

Preston accused him of needing therapy, of being an emotional wreck. Paul blew up at his twin every time Preston urged him to get help. Unless someone could spin back the hands of time, and undo what had been done to him, Paul knew there was no helping him. It made him angry that Preston thought there was anything good left in him.

Tonight he'd proven to himself at least that there wasn't.

Paul ran down the sidewalk, uncaring of which way he was going—he just had to escape. He could hear other footsteps behind him, rapid ones, sounds of pursuit. There weren't too many people out after midnight on a weekday. Add to that the fact that it was close to freezing out and drizzling. It didn't make for the kind of weather people enjoyed walking in.

Paul slipped, his right leg almost giving out as his heel came down on something slick. He just managed to right himself in time to avoid being grabbed. He knew it because, while he didn't waste time looking back, he felt the jerk of a hand grabbing his shirt. There was a jolt of resistance then Paul was off again, powering his legs, pumping his arms to get him moving faster and faster.

He had news for whoever was chasing him—he could run forever. Or until his heart burst, Paul didn't particularly care, but he wouldn't let them catch him. Death held more appeal than to be a captive for any amount of time at all.

Paul darted across an empty intersection. He refused to look back, to give whoever was chasing him the satisfaction of believing Paul was afraid they'd catch him. He wasn't, they wouldn't.

His heels struck the pavement hard enough to cause bolts of pain to shoot up his shins, but Paul didn't care. Little things registered in his awareness. The street lamps weren't all functioning, casting shadows more than light. The temperature seemed to be dropping even though he was sweating. There were less footsteps and panting behind him.

That last one was the important thing to note. Paul was still running hard and wasn't even winded. He ran every day, often times until he had to stop or collapse. This sprinting was nothing.

Further down the street, the lampposts were all out. Paul knew the area well enough. He never went to a bar or club without memorising the layout of the neighbourhood, without walking through it a time or two first. Being prepared, aware, alert—those things saved people's lives. Paul had learnt his lesson about not being any of those things.

He took a right between two brick buildings. From the sounds of it, there was only one person chasing him still. Paul was about to lose him. He darted around the dumpsters and the homeless man passed out on the ground. At least the guy or woman had blankets, which was more than a lot of the homeless people had.

There'd been a time when Paul had thought he'd do something great in the world, help people somehow, but all those dreams were dead now. They hadn't left Paul, though. No, they were decaying inside him, the rot from them taking pieces of him with it.

Paul snorted at his melancholy musings. He had someone trying to catch him and he was waxing philosophical. Well, whatever, it wasn't slowing him down any.

At the end of the alley, a ten-foot-high chain-link fence topped with barbed wire presented a minor obstacle. Paul added more power behind his running, then he leapt and caught the fencing right below the wire on top of it. Yeah, he practised escaping as often as he could. People probably thought he was just a Parkour nut, running and climbing, manoeuvring in ways that most people couldn't. He wasn't. Paul was just determined to survive.

He cleared the fence easily and landed into an immediate roll. Not once did he stop moving as he came up and took off running again. Someone, or something, hit the fence behind him. Paul grinned. Regular people couldn't keep up with him.

But a shifter would have already caught you.

"Fuck you," Paul rasped to himself. He took another running leap and kicked off from one building. As soon as he twisted and his feet hit the building opposite of the first one, Paul contorted and stretched as he shoved off again. He reached out and caught the ledge of the rooftop and pulled himself up, using his body's forward momentum in his favour. He was on the rooftop in seconds.

Only then did he pause to look down at whoever had thought to catch him. The guy hadn't even made it over the fence. Paul chuckled and took off. His amusement quickly died when he thought about the man he'd struck.

Paul replayed that instant over and over in his head as he made his way back towards his side of town. He lived approximately nine miles from the bar he'd just left, and by his estimates, he still had about seven miles to go.

He touched his palm. There was no tenderness there, not that it'd have meant anything if he'd been sore. Killing a man with a hit to the throat didn't always take a lot of brute strength.

He hadn't meant to seriously hurt anyone, he'd just wanted to be free. Being grabbed, it tended to unnerve him and send him into defensive mode. There'd been that hungry, mean look in the man's eyes, the kind of look that Paul had seen before and had meant he wasn't going to walk away unhurt.

But the lighting had been bad, and he could have been wrong, could have asked the guy to leave him the fuck alone.

God, he couldn't deal with that right then. Paul scrubbed his hands over his face. His stubble scraped at his palms. Too many thoughts were trying to take precedence in his head, and he couldn't sort any of them out.

Paul shook himself from top to toes. He looked out from the rooftop. *Still no stars or moon.* The drizzle had stopped, but he only then became aware of being wet and cold. His teeth chattered and Paul clamped them tightly together.

Going back to the bar was out. He'd have to watch the news, and if… Paul closed his eyes and reached for what little of his soul remained. If he'd hurt that guy badly, if he'd killed him, then he'd turn himself in.

And be a prisoner again, because I was a fucking fool. He didn't know if he could go through with it, but he did know he wouldn't be able to live with himself if he didn't.

Chapter Two

Paul thrust in again and sealed his lips shut against the moan knocking at his teeth. The guy sucking his dick moaned plenty enough for both of them, anyway. As soon as Paul's load was shot, he pulled out of the man's mouth. With a flick of his wrist, he had the condom off and tossed on the ground.

"Thanks," he muttered while he tucked his penis away. He zipped up his pants and glanced at the man still kneeling. He was jacking himself off with harsh, fast strokes, and for one moment, Paul wanted to squat beside him and take over, to bring him off and just be a part of something, someone, other than himself.

He didn't. Instead Paul turned and walked away. They both knew the score. Neither of them cared about the other's feelings. The guy had got off on sucking Paul, on making Paul lose it and blow a wad in his mouth. He didn't want or need Paul for the rest of it, which was just how Paul liked his sex to go. If there was a little twinge of jealousy in his chest, a little pinch of longing for something more, Paul ruthlessly stomped it down.

His brother Preston had found a man perfect for him—a 'mate', Preston called the guy. Paul just called him a shifter, though Nischal wasn't a wolf shifter and he didn't seem like a bad guy. Not that Paul had hung around him long enough to be certain. He wouldn't stay around any kind of shifter longer than he absolutely had to.

But Preston and Nischal were so close, like two halves of a whole reunited—Paul snorted as he strode down the sidewalk. He was becoming a fanciful idiot.

He ran a hand over his buzzed hair. After a week with no cops knocking on his door, and no reports of the assault he'd committed showing up in the papers or on the TV news, Paul had given in to the urging to whack off his hair. He'd wanted to as soon as he'd got home that night, but he'd stopped himself then.

Part of him had wanted to bleach out his hair again and try to get rid of some of the freckles like he used to. But he didn't, because he knew that was the shitty, cowardly part of himself speaking. That part wanted him to run if he'd really hurt or killed that guy. Run, rather than face jail time.

Paul still had some honour in his soul, he guessed. More likely, he just hadn't wanted to let Preston down. So he'd made himself wait until a week had passed. At that point, he assumed he wasn't going to get arrested, and changing his appearance a little wasn't a means to try to keep from being ID'd.

Now his hair was barely even there. Paul scrubbed at it again, liking the bristly feeling of it beneath his palm. There was no need to style the short strands. No one could grab them and use his hair as a means to hurt or hold him for their pleasure.

Pleasure. What was that, really? Paul couldn't remember really enjoying anything anymore. He knew he had done once—he'd been a happy enough kid, and didn't have a fuckton of woeful tales to tell, up until his parents freaked over the whole gay thing. Still, it was as if the past year and a half had eradicated the part of his brain that could feel pleasure, or remember it.

Yeah, he'd just shot his wad with some guy, but that had been more of an instinctive sensation. He'd come because his body had demanded it, not because he'd been so into it he couldn't stop the ecstasy from bursting up from his balls.

That being the scenario, he questioned why he even bothered. Paul huffed as he batted away some bug drawn by the street lamps. He bothered because he would go fucking crazy if he sat in his shithole of an apartment and thought about what had happened to him.

He bothered because he needed to be the one in control, to prove to himself that he wasn't weak or hopelessly damaged—

"Stop it," he muttered to himself. A quick check proved him to be alone on the street corner. He pulled his phone from his shirt pocket and checked the time. Not yet midnight, and he had nothing to do but wander around or go back and watch TV. A movie was out of the question.

The two part-time jobs he had didn't pay enough for splurges such as that. He was lucky he could make the rent and utilities. Being a waiter wasn't bringing him in much *dinero*. He never got the big tips like some of the other people he worked with.

The suggestion that he smile more often always fell flat with him. He'd deal with scraping by before he faked being some happy idiot for money.

As he continued walking towards his place, Paul became aware of the eerie sensation of being watched. It made the skin on his nape tingle and itch, like he had spiders running over it. He fisted his hands to keep from reaching back to rub at it.

At the same time, he tried to look around as unobtrusively as possible. There wasn't a single person in sight, but that didn't mean a damn thing.

There'd been wolf shifters who had hurt him. Paul hadn't ever told the FBI agents that part, because why the hell would they believe him? He'd have been locked away in some psych ward for eternity. No, he'd described the men who'd used him as regular ol' humans, but most of them weren't.

And they'd want to find him, wouldn't they?

Paul shivered despite his best effort not to. He hadn't heard from the FBI agent who'd been in charge of his case in months. As far as he knew, the human trafficking ring he'd fallen prey to was still functioning on some level. Otherwise, he'd have been called in for interviews, for trials and stuff, wouldn't he?

Which meant there were still a half dozen or more freaks on the loose, ones who could turn into wolves and rip him to shreds. *Why the hell did I think I needed to go out tonight?*

He'd been safe for months. No one had tried to do anything to him except for the jackass at the club the week before. All the precautions he'd taken at first, he'd been so careful, and now he realised he'd been letting those safety measures slip.

Why did I do that? Paul increased the speed of his strides in minute increments, all the while becoming more aware of the feeling that someone was watching him. He didn't want to appear to run, but he wasn't going to make it easy to be caught, and he sure as hell wasn't going to be anyone else's pet, ever again.

Paul glanced around at the street corner. He thought he saw movement in the alley to his right, but that couldn't have been whoever was watching him. They wouldn't have been around him when the sensation first began. There were a few places open on the next block or two. He'd enter the first one and see if there wasn't another way to exit from it.

Maybe he was being paranoid, but he shouldn't have ever stopped being paranoid in the first place. He knew how dangerous shifters were. He had the scars, inside and out, to prove it.

As he crossed the street, Paul kept his gaze mobile, checking his surroundings. He began to truly question his sanity—not about the shifters, he knew they were real. But about whether or not he was possibly suicidal.

The answer had his gut cramping. Whether he wanted to admit it or not, he'd been taking deadly risks, going out to seedy clubs and hooking up with men who, for all he knew, could turn into some kind of animal.

Yeah, I think I have some problems. Jesus Christ, I hope Preston doesn't say 'I told you so'.

Paul didn't question why it'd taken him months to come around to the fact that he was fucked up. Anyone who had been through what he had would be at least as screwy as he was. Now he just hoped he had the chance to do something about the realisation.

As he neared a jazz club, Paul turned around and looked behind him. Fuck it if whoever was after him knew he'd caught on. Fuck his own carelessness. Paul suddenly, fervently, wanted to live, and that wasn't going to happen much longer if he kept going the way he was going.

No one was behind him, yet he still felt like prey. Paul spun around and collided with a hard, sweat-scented chest.

"Well, well, if it isn't the pet who got away," a familiar deep voice rumbled.

Paul began to shake as he was embraced by arms strong enough to break his back. He couldn't swallow—his mouth had gone dry.

"We're going to have so much fun, pretty pet," the shifter rumbled. "I'll have to punish you for cutting off your hair, of course."

Paul's chin was gripped painfully and his head forced up. He couldn't help but meet Terence's dark eyes. Paul bit his tongue trying to keep back the whimper of fear bubbling out of him, but it was no use. Terence could smell it anyway, just like he'd smell the piss if Paul's bladder gave way, which it might. It wouldn't have been the first time that terror or pain had caused such a humiliation.

"Such a pretty boy," Terence crooned in a soft voice that sent chills down Paul's spine. "No hair, though, so I'll have to fit you with a bit, don't you think?"

"That's a lot of effort for some stupid human piece of ass you plan to kill," said another familiar voice from behind Terence. "He's not that good a fuck."

Terence smiled and tightened his hold on Paul's chin. Tears leaked from Paul's eyes. He was too late to save himself.

"He's a better fuck than you are, Pat," Terence said, still watching Paul. "And the way he reacts to pain, it's so beautiful. Breaking this pet has always been better than any sex I've had with you, or anyone else."

Paul closed his eyes, unable to keep them open. Pat would kill him for sure, slowly, as slowly as possible. No doubt that was why Terence was egging his lover on.

"I think you're both two fucked-up pups," a third, unknown voice said.

Before another word was said, Pat made a muffled sound. Terence shoved Paul away so hard he bounced when he hit the ground. Paul couldn't see for a moment. Everything was blurry and his head throbbed from the impact with the sidewalk. He could make out figures scuffling, he thought. He blinked and pushed himself up to a sitting position. His entire body ached.

Rapid blinking helped clear his vision just in time for him to see blood on the sidewalk. The three men—shifters, at least the two of them—were fighting at the entrance to the alley. Two of them were, Paul corrected himself. Pat was still and unmoving on the ground.

Paul didn't hang around. He got up, stumbling into a sprint that carried him away from the scary happenings.

He didn't know how he managed to get to his apartment, but he did. Paul scurried up the steps, taking out a roach or two along the way. He tugged his keys from his pants pocket and unlocked the shitty deadbolt on his door. The lock on the knob always stuck, and tonight was no exception. Paul cursed as he jiggled the key, then finally he was able to open the door and get inside.

Despite locking the door, he wasn't safe. Paul knew it. The shifters had found him, and someone—who the fuck, he didn't know—had found Terence and Pat. Paul hoped they were dead, but he had no idea if they were. Even so, there was the matter of the third guy, whoever he was.

It could have been one of many men, shifters, who'd been allowed to fuck him by his—Paul stopped himself. He wouldn't call that bastard his owner, not anymore.

He had to move past it all, somehow. Paul leaned his back against the door then slid down until he landed with a thump. It jarred his body, reminding him that he'd had a nasty fall earlier and he hurt all over. A shower was in order, and as many pain pills as he could take without killing himself.

Except that would mean he had to get up. Paul's heart raced erratically at the idea of leaving the door unguarded. It was stupid. He couldn't keep a shifter from breaking it down, but somehow, his brain kept telling him that if he got up, the door would be imploded by a rabid wolf. Images of himself with his throat torn out, entrails strewn all over the small apartment, wouldn't leave his mind.

Paul gasped. He couldn't get a decent breath. His head felt light and grey dots invaded his vision. Sweat popped up all over his body, chilling him even as he felt heated from the inside out.

Then the shaking began. Paul had thought he'd hit the ground hard earlier, but his body was bordering on convulsing. It caused his teeth to clack loudly together and his back and head to hit the door repeatedly. He tried to bend his neck, get his head down some. Whether it helped or not, he couldn't say, because he couldn't breathe—then his world went dark.

Chapter Three

"How is it two states can be side by side, yet be so damned different?"

Justice Chalmers glanced at his sister Vivian before returning his full attention to the road. Traffic was moderate on I-25 since they were on the outskirts of Denver. If they'd been an hour later, they'd have got hung up in traffic, but they'd hit Denver at nine a.m. so it hadn't been too bad. It hadn't been great, either.

"Arizona sure doesn't look anything like this, at least not our part of it," Justice conceded. "I wouldn't live anywhere else than Phoenix, though. Suits me."

Viv snorted and he just knew she was rolling her eyes. "Of course it does. I love that place, but there sure are some, er, different people there."

"Snob," he chided. "There are *different* people everywhere. Otherwise it'd be pretty damn boring. Bunch of uptight pricks wearing ties and shit…"

"Yes, I know, and for a psychologist, that did sound rather snobby." She patted his arm. "As it happens, I love your eclectic town and friends, just like I love you, bro."

Justice barely kept from rolling his eyes. "Drop the 'bro', Viv. There's nothing worse than a prep trying to sound hip."

"Now who's being the snob?" she said with entirely too much glee. "Hey there, pot. Labels suck."

"Yeah, they do, but not being able to tease and joke sucks too." Justice signalled for the exit that would take them to his grandma's place. "Stop being a stick-in-the-mud, sis."

Viv tipped her nose up. Justice saw the movement in his peripheral vision and he grinned. His little sister was so much fun to tease, especially now that she'd got her license to practise psychology.

"Bet you never thought this is how you'd start your business off," he told her as he checked to see if it was safe to merge.

"Helping family wasn't on my list of expectations, no," she admitted, "But only because I assumed it'd only include our blood family and their mates. You know how proud shifters are, and men? Right. Men are less likely than a woman to ask for help or even admit they need it. To be fair, I'm not exactly helping a family member, directly."

"No, but you're helping the brother of one of our long-lost relatives' mate." Justice had to run that over in his head to make sure he hadn't bungled it. "Did that make sense?"

Viv snickered then patted him again. "Talking yourself in circles again? Yes, I do believe I know who I'm helping."

Justice didn't say anything else, having enough sense to know he'd come close to insulting his sister already. Still, he wondered what the newly-ish discovered family members would look like. Justice had missed the annual family reunion—and by God, his grandma had bitched him out good for that—so he hadn't met the newbies, Nischal and Sabin. No last names as far as he knew. They'd been raised in the mountains of Nepal by their mother until her death. Isolated, except for an old guy who'd befriended them later.

Before they were caught and used as a sideshow attraction to draw in victims for some kind of human trafficking scheme. Justice wasn't real clear on how all that had happened, but Nischal and Sabin were related to Grandma Marybeth on their mother's side, and therefore, they were family no matter how many times removed they might be as cousins to Justice and Viv.

And Nischal had found his mate, a short little ginger man by the name of Preston. That was about all Justice knew. He'd seen pictures of the new family members and Preston a while back. They seemed happy.

But Preston had a twin who was having problems. "You think—and please don't get mad, sis, I'm just asking out of concern for you..." He really was, because if she failed, and something went wrong, Viv would never forgive herself. She'd already had one severe trauma in her life. Justice hadn't been around to help her through it, but he'd make sure she wasn't hurt again.

He cleared his throat then continued, "Are you ready for something as intense as this will be? I mean, this Paul guy, he was kidnapped, sold, abused— sexually and probably in any other way possible. By shifters."

Viv sighed and he risked a longer look at her since the road was all but abandoned to them. She wasn't mad at him. That was sadness pulling the corners of her mouth down.

"Viv—"

"I have to try," she said. "Paul can't go to a human psychologist and talk to them. He can't confide in one, and he's a mess, of course he is. From what I've been told…" Viv shook her head. "I can't spill his secrets, that's unethical. He needs help, and I'm going to be there for him if he'll let me. Anything else is out of the question."

The words dug into Justice's conscience like sharp little daggers. He gripped the wheel tighter. He'd said it before, but it bore repeating. "I'm sorry I wasn't there for you, Viv. I wish the military would have let me come home—"

Viv cut him off. "This isn't about what happened to me, and really, what happened to me? Nothing compared to that poor man we hit." Her voice wavered and she sniffled. "Young, dumb, drinking and driving. We all knew better, Jus. We just thought nothing bad would ever happen to us."

Justice had to bite back any more protests. If he'd been home instead of in Iraq a half-dozen years ago, Viv would never have been out running around with a bad crowd.

Not a bad crowd. Just dumb kids. It wasn't like he hadn't done his share of idiotic things when he'd been a minor. He'd got drunk lots of times, even smoked a few joints. He'd never driven drunk, and neither had Viv.

And yes, he'd ridden with a friend driving who had been too intoxicated to be at the wheel. He could honestly say, there but for the grace of God… Which was why he'd have known what Viv and her friends were up to back then. *If* he'd been around. But he hadn't been, and her best friend had died in the same wreck that had killed a father of three who'd been pumping gas.

"It's true, what they say," Viv said, interrupting his musings.

"What's true? Or what do they say?" He wasn't sure there was a difference in what he was asking. Sometimes Viv confused him, or he confused himself.

"There's this general consensus that people go into psychology and psychiatry because they really want to know what's wrong with themselves."

"There's nothing wrong with you," Justice said a little louder than he meant to. He winced, sent his sister an apologetic look. "There's not. You were doing the same dumb shit teenagers have been doing forever. Kids aren't known for their stellar judgement."

"I know that, but what happened has affected me, and, in a way, impaired me." Viv slapped the dashboard. "You know it. Otherwise I would be able to drive, and I can't. I just can't. Even sitting in the driver's seat sends me into a panic attack."

Justice had seen some fighting in Iraq. He knew how the memories of torn bodies could haunt a person. Being a teenager, sitting in the front seat and seeing the car strike someone who then flew up into the windshield—that had to cause as many scars as the ones he carried around in his head.

"I'm happy to drive you. Grandma would have my nuts in a vise if I didn't come along, anyway."

Viv made a gagging sound. "Gross, bro. Do *not* mention Grandma and your testicles in the same sentence. In fact, *I* don't want to hear about—"

"Sorry. Honest slip." Sometimes he just blurted out shit like he was talking to one of his Marine buddies. A decade of serving in the military had left him with habits that weren't all good. "Grandma Marybeth will twist my ear off then thump my nose with the bloody cartilage."

Viv's laughter was a little forced, but it still warmed him inside.

"You want to stop in town before we hit up the family compound?" he asked about an hour later when they were close to Holton. From there, it was only a fifteen- or twenty-minute drive to their Grandma's.

"You make it sound like some weird cult."

"Aren't all cults weird?" Justice would have thought so. "It's part of what makes them a cult, because they don't fit in with societal norms."

"I'm impressed," Viv said with enough approval in her voice that he knew she meant it. "You're smarter than you look."

Justice laughed and waggled his eyebrows. "Brains and handsome, too. It always surprises people."

Viv looked just like him, well as much like him as she could while still retaining the feminine beauty version of his looks. She was taller than him, even, six-two to his six feet even. She wasn't the tallest woman in the family, not at all. There were plenty of them, though there were more petite women, too. But Viv had broad shoulders, and a muscular build that, when combined with her curves, had Justice growling at gawkers every time they went out.

He'd been raised better than to treat any woman like a sex object. The same went for men. Once he'd figured out he was gay and told his parents, he was given the same talking to about respecting men. Call him old-fashioned, but the lessons had stuck. Fucking around had its place in life, but Justice tried not to treat anyone like a piece of meat.

"You know, I would like to stop in town," Viv said as they were approaching the Holton sign. "I forgot to bring pads—"

"I'm not listening," Justice hollered, holding one hand to his right ear. "La-la-la-la!"

A hard pop to his shoulder almost sent his head against the glass. He put his hand back on the steering wheel. "Beating me up isn't going to encourage me to stop."

"I'll just talk about how my last period was so—"

"Fine!" Justice signalled to turn onto Main. "You win. Please don't subject me to the gory details. I already have to deal with your PMS."

"At least I have an excuse for my moods. You just act like an ass at times. Besides, I'm moving out next month. You're going to miss me *and* my hormonal rages."

"Right." Justice dragged the word out. "I'll miss you, but as for the other, I can just drag my nails down a chalkboard for days or something."

"Jerk," Viv said before laughing. "I wasn't that bad."

Justice parked in one of the many open spots by the post office. "Uh, yeah, Viv, you could be. You screamed at me for leaving the seat up when you were the one who did it, and before you bitch about having to clean the toilet, it was your turn. That whole deal was totally not my fault."

She shrugged. "I'm sure there've been plenty of other times I could have yelled at you and didn't, like when you used all the mouthwash or put the milk container in the fridge empty. Consider it a delayed reaction."

He knew when he was beat. At least she hadn't nailed him over using the last of the toilet paper in the middle of the night and forgetting to warn her. Then again, she'd shrieked at him for a week over that. Maybe he'd already paid his dues for it.

"I'm going to go to the pharmacy first, then I want to hit up the new boutique and the antique store, too." Viv glanced at her phone. "We told Grandma we'd be there by three, so we have time. Is that okay?"

"Yeah, it's good. You want me to go with you?" He didn't want to, but he wouldn't abandon his sister.

Viv waved him off. "No, you'll just whine when I'm trying to shop. Go to the hardware store, or the diner. I'll meet you back here at two-thirty."

"Deal." Justice waited for his sister to get out. He pulled out of the parking space. The gas tank needed filling, and he'd always hated doing it with Viv in the car. She said it was fine, but he was afraid she was reliving that wreck every time he pumped gas.

There was a gas station on the outskirt of town, the opposite side from where they came into Holton. Justice pulled up to a pump. The place was actually decent-sized, with numerous pumps and a good dozen eighteen-wheelers parked in the large lot to the left of the store.

He got out and took care of fuelling up. When he finished, he stretched and his lower back popped. He walked around the front of the car. The smell of gasoline was burning his nose and he sneezed. One of the downsides of being a snow leopard shifter—his olfactory senses were very...sensitive. He could sniff out things no human ever could hope to, which was a plus at times. Not always. Bad odours hit him a lot harder than a regular person, and some things could send him into a sneezing fit.

Gas didn't always do it, but sometimes it did. He sneezed repeatedly. His eyes teared up and Justice had to swipe at his cheeks. No doubt he made an amusing figure to anyone who might be watching. There he was, a big, muscular guy with tears streaming down his cheeks.

Eyes burning, Justice covered his face with his hands and took a few steady breaths. When he didn't sneeze again, he wiped his face off with the sleeve of his shirt. His nose was running, and he bet he looked a sight. Tissues would be a blessing, but he knew there were none in the car.

Justice wiped his face again. Hopefully he had got all the tears off. It didn't matter that he'd had a little allergy-like attack. Walking into a gas station-slash-truck stop looking like he'd been crying? Not something he ever wanted to do.

If his bladder hadn't decided to start aching, he'd have just left. As it was, going inside was kind of necessary.

Justice's nose burned and he felt kind of flushed, warm and tingly as he entered the building. It was weird, and he wondered if he'd managed to catch some kind of cold or something, even though he'd always been healthy. Stopping a few feet from the door, he tried to analyse what he was experiencing.

It reminded him of the times he'd been afraid, when he'd feared for his and his friends' lives in Iraq, except he wasn't actually scared. His body was reacting the same way, though. His heart was beating too fast, slapping out an erratic beat. His pulse was too high, and he was breathing wrong. Short, shallow breaths— maybe he was having a flashback.

Except he wasn't back in Iraq, not in his mind. He was standing there in the gas station, drawing an odd look here and there.

Must have inhaled too many gas fumes. Although why that was making his entire groin tingle was beyond him. Justice started for the restrooms. Each step he took made his symptoms worse. Added to that, his damned cock was getting hard, and that part of him was big enough that it'd be really noticeable in no time at all. Plus, pissing with a raging hard-on was damn near impossible.

If he remembered right, this place had a large men's room, and a more private 'Family' restroom for parents to take children into. Awful as it was, Justice thought he was going to have to slip into that one and beat off. He was randier than a bull in a pen-full of cows in season.

Justice untucked his shirt as he neared the restroom. He pulled the front down over his straining erection just as a short, white-haired man stepped in front of him.

Every atom in Justice's body went on alert. The urge to grab the man and fuck him right then and there was almost overwhelming. His leopard was all for it, snarling and on the verge of demanding to be loosed.

Serving a decade in the military had helped Justice to hone his self-control to a fine point. He firmly stomped down the leopard's demands. Sweat coated his brow as he tried to keep from ogling the smaller man's ass.

He didn't have that much control. It was too fine of a butt to ignore, encased in faded jeans that looked thin and worn yet moulded perfectly to those firm, round buttocks. Justice thought he'd never seen such a perfect derriere.

Then the man glanced back over his shoulder at Justice. The hunger in those green-blue eyes stabbed at him. The stranger licked his lips and turned a little more. He raked Justice with a wanton look that sent the lust pumping through his veins.

An arched eyebrow was all it took. The man turned back around and sauntered to the family restroom. Justice didn't even hesitate to follow. He needed, more than he ever had before. His body was in control, and he didn't question what was happening. He ached for the stranger.

Never had he been so drawn to a man. Justice's mouth watered to taste him. There was no hesitation on either of their parts to enter the restroom. As soon as Justice was inside, the stranger shoved him up against the door and twisted the lock.

This close, Justice could smell the traces of bleach in the man's hair. He noticed the darker eyebrows, too. Before he could speak, short, thick fingers were pressed against his lips. Justice frowned and looked into those pretty eyes.

Confusion and need shone clearly in their depths, but so did something close to anger. Justice knew with a certainty that if he spoke, he'd be left with an aching erection and a shitload of regret. He gave a terse nod. The man seemed to relax just a bit and he traced the outline of Justice's lips.

Justice didn't need any more of a hint than that. He dropped to his knees and reached for the other man's belt buckle.

It surprised him that he was allowed to unfasten the buckle and jeans. There was something so controlled about the stranger, so tightly wound. Justice looked up at him and the strangest thing happened. His heart ached with a pain that wasn't his own. Need swamped him at the same time, doubling in him.

Something was happening between them, and it was unlike anything Justice had ever experienced before. He could feel things he couldn't quite comprehend the why of. The man now fishing out his stiff cock had been hurt, was scared, *needed* him.

As much as Justice wanted to say something, he had the distinct feeling that what he was doing, kneeling, waiting for that cock to be pushed past his lips, was what the stranger needed. He almost objected when the man slid a condom onto his fat, veiny cock, but Justice really wasn't going to explain why such a thing wasn't necessary. Shifters didn't contract human diseases, and he fucking hated the taste of latex, but he'd do anything to have that cock in his mouth.

Justice locked gazes with the stranger. He licked his lips, then parted them. The man cupped his chin and nape. A look of what might have been tenderness flickered over the harsh lines of the guy's face before a neutral expression settled in place. Justice reached for the man's shaft and helped guide it to where he needed it to be.

Latex was possibly the worst thing he'd ever tasted, but hearing the soft gasp slip from the other man was more than worth it. Feeling his mouth being stretched wide for that thick cock, that was way past worth it, too. Despite the desire to keep his eyes open, Justice felt his lids drooping. He gave up trying to watch as his mouth was filled.

Justice tongued every vein he found and sucked like his life depended on it. He cupped the smooth, hot balls. That got him another gasp, this one louder, with a husky tone to it, like a word almost slipped past the man.

It made Justice more determined to hear the stranger's voice. He rolled the balls in his hand and let go of the man's cock. Doing so allowed that thick length to be pushed into his throat. Justice swallowed eagerly. At the same time, he gently pushed the man's nuts up close to his body.

"Fuck."

That one rasped word spurred Justice on. He moaned and bobbed his head, up and down, sucking so hard his jaws ached. That was of no concern, not when he drew more softly uttered curses from the man. Justice's own dick ached to be touched, but he was too busy to mess with it just then. He could get there, though.

Dragging one hand down a well-muscled thigh, even though it was covered in denim, got Justice another uttered oath. He grinned, or tried to. The stranger grunted and began to thrust, harder, faster. The balls in Justice's hand drew up tight.

Oh no you don't, not without me! The man gasped so loudly it was almost a shout. Justice ripped open his own jeans and got a hand on his cock, figuring the other guy was about to come. He fisted his length and started pumping right away, grateful for the pre-cum that helped slick that delicate skin.

He swallowed when his throat was breached again, and pressed the man's balls a little more firmly. The man's groan sounded like it was torn from his core. Justice opened his eyes in time to see him tip his head back and moan again.

Jerking like he was being poked with a cattle prod repeatedly, the stranger shot his load into the condom. Justice wanted to taste that spunk so bad. He twisted his hand around his cock, desperate for release. His gut burned with the need for it. A glance at those pretty eyes, and Justice knew he was on his own in the pursuit of pleasure.

It should have pissed him off. He wasn't a selfish lover and didn't care to mess around with someone who was.

Yet he still wanted the stranger, wanted to mark him with cum and bites, scratches and—

What the fuck is wrong with me?

Justice barely got the thought out before he was being urged to his feet. The other man had him under the arm pits and was trying to get him to rise.

Somehow, Justice managed to stand. Immediately another hand was on his cock, stroking, slightly dragging nails over that most sensitive skin. Justice looked down to watch his and the stranger's hands work in tandem. His own skin was a medium brown, tanned from years in the sun. The other man's was pale, almost white but for the pink tint to it, and the freckles. There were soft, golden hairs all over the guy's forearm, too.

A twist that rubbed his frenulum just right had Justice trembling as his climax rushed to the surface. He gulped, wishing he could shout and grab onto the sexy stud in front of him.

Then that stud reached out and pinched Justice's left tit, hard. Pain shot out from around the nub and sent flames of ecstasy licking up Justice's dick.

Justice panted as his head spun. His vision went blurry and he thrust mindlessly into their hands. Cum spurted from his slit, and he moaned with every jet of it.

By the time he finished, his knees didn't seem to be all that trustworthy. In fact, he thought he might just fall over. As it was, Justice leaned against the wall and tried to calm his body down. His dick hadn't even started to go soft.

"Hey, Paul? You in there?" someone called out as they banged on the door a minute later. "Paul?"

"Just a minute," the man—presumably Paul—rasped back at the person who asked. "I'll be out to the truck. Don't pressure me, bub." He pulled off the condom then dropped it in the toilet before zipping his cock away.

Those green-blue eyes were focused on him the entire time Paul spoke, but Justice's brain had kind of shuddered to a halt. *Paul. Paul who looked an awful lot like Preston, at least in the pictures I've seen. Change that hair to orange, and… Jesus fuck, what did we just do?*

Paul nudged him aside and left Justice standing there, wondering how badly he'd just fucked everything up, not only for himself and the man who'd just rocked his world, but for Viv.

Chapter Four

Paul had been trying, he really had. He'd been so good, not that he'd had any choice, really. Ever since he'd had that...that breakdown in his apartment two weeks ago, he'd not even beat off. Maybe part of that was humiliation—apparently sometime during his crazy spell, he'd called Preston.

Preston kept telling him not to call it that, but what the fuck. Paul knew he was broken. His brain was damaged from what had happened to him, as surely as if someone had taken that grey stuff out and smacked it with a hammer a time or two.

No one with any sense took the risks he had. Hell, he hadn't even used condoms all the time. It had just depended on his mood, on the darkness that had weighed on him. So far he'd tested clean, but what about the next time he did something unquestionably stupid?

Did he want to die? *Sometimes, yes. I just want it to all stop.*

The memories haunted him, in his sleep more often than not, but sometimes while he was awake, trying not to think. Something little would trigger a flashback, a word or even a sound, a scent. There was no hope for him.

And he'd just practically attacked a man in a public restroom, with Preston not nearly far enough away. Jesus, he didn't think he could be any more fucked up.

But he'd seen that big guy, and everything inside Paul had done a kind of shimmy, like a pup greeting its owner after they'd been apart all day. Paul had fairly wagged with an unfamiliar sensation. He'd seemed to have no control as he'd approached the guy, then he'd lured him into the restroom.

He'd have liked to have heard that voice. Paul had been afraid he'd crumble, though why he didn't have a clue. Silence had just been necessary. His heart had raced as he touched the man's lips. There was something familiar about the green and gold-flecked eyes, not that he could place it just then. His body was still humming with the aftermath of a pleasure so intense he wanted to weep from it.

Instead he picked out a candy bar and went over to the cashier to pay for it. Preston watched him, frowning slightly. Paul wasn't going to tell him how he'd fucked up. He was already the cause of too much worry and regret in Preston's life. It probably would have been better if he'd just been killed instead of found.

"Stop it," he muttered to himself. He got so sick of his pity-partying.

"Excuse me?" the cashier snapped.

Paul glanced at the burly woman behind the counter. She looked like she could and would snap him in two.

"Sorry." He didn't sound like it, but whatever. He hadn't been talking to her anyway, and he wasn't going to be scared.

Then he was, but not of her. He felt the gaze on him like a touch, trying to claim him. *Where the hell did that thought come from?*

Paul stiffened before he could stop himself, then he relaxed as he took his change handed to him by the glaring cashier. Guilt prodded him to say, "I was just muttering to myself. Sorry." It sounded sincere enough that she quit looking like she wanted to deck him.

"Have a good day," she even told him. Paul thought he said something appropriate back to her. With the chaos in his body, he couldn't be sure.

That same happy, wag-wag-wag sensation was bubbling up in him again. Paul brought his hand up to his nose before he could censor the movement. He sniffed and inhaled the scent of cock and spunk. It made him shiver, made his buttocks clench with a need he hadn't acknowledged in more months than he could remember. Want curled in his groin, stiffening his cock.

Jesus, he was becoming a sex addict! Paul lowered his hand and shoved it in his pocket as he walked towards the door. Preston had finally gone outside, thank God. Paul didn't think he could disguise the lust spiralling through him. He sure couldn't hide the erection that shouldn't have been possible. He'd just come minutes before.

Yet his shaft was as hard as the pavement beneath his feet as he left the store. The door opened up behind him, and he just knew who was following him. It wasn't fear that made his heart leap. The man wasn't going to hurt him.

What the hell is happening? I want... Paul refused to admit what he wanted. Going there wasn't an option. He was never letting anyone that close to him again.

Which didn't explain why he slowed his steps. Preston and Nischal were waiting in the truck. *Shit.* Paul realised belatedly that he should have scrubbed off in the restroom. Nischal would smell the cum on him. *Damned shifter. God damn it!*

Shame burned in him, leaching out to warm his cheeks uncomfortably. Paul stumbled and would have fallen had he not been grabbed by the shoulder from behind.

"Hey, you okay?"

"Oh God," Paul rasped before he could bite his tongue. That deep, rumbly voice almost made him come in his jeans. He jerked away from the man's hold.

"Sorry. I was just trying—"

"Let go of him!"

Paul groaned and closed his eyes the second he heard Preston shout. He was released instantly.

"I was just trying to keep him from falling."

Paul glanced behind him to see the man holding both hands up in the air, chest-height. He turned back in time to see Nischal jogging after Preston. Paul closed his eyes and groaned. *This is about to become a real clusterfuck.* Opening his eyes, he tried to think up an explanation, but really, short of 'I jumped this big, sexy stud as soon as I could', there wasn't much he could say.

"Paul, come on."

Paul cringed at the pity in his brother's voice. Maybe that wasn't what Preston intended, but it was what Paul heard.

"I'm fine," he snapped. "Let's go."

But Preston had other ideas as he walked over. "Hey, are you related to the Travis family?"

Oh shit. Paul swung around and gaped at the man he'd got off with—that he'd helped to get off. For the first time in ages, Paul had touched someone else and enjoyed it.

He didn't hear the words the man spoke. Instead he took in the long nose, the high cheekbones and the firm, square chin. That hair that had looked almost black inside was a dark auburn in the sunlight. And his build…

"Fuck," Paul spat, disgust trying to rear up over what he'd just done, and who he'd done it with. "Go back to the truck, Nischal."

"I smell…" Nischal began. Paul bumped him hard as he strode quickly towards the truck. Nischal's grunt didn't quite muddle his words. "Cum. Did you fuck Paul?"

Paul was pretty sure he'd just fucked himself.

* * * *

Justice had known he'd fucked up, but it was quickly sinking in just how badly he'd done so as he answered Nischal's question.

"No," Justice said, watching the way Paul's ass flexed beneath his jeans as he all but ran off.

"Bullshit," Nischal growled. "I don't care that you're related to me somehow, you can't have Paul!"

Those words caused an uproar with Justice's leopard. The beast raged in him, demanding a chance to gnaw some manners into Nischal. Justice narrowed his eyes at the man as Preston took off after his brother.

"You would do well to shut up about now," Justice warned. Normally he was more patient, less of a dick, but he was barely refraining from shifting and going after Nischal's throat. No one was going to tell him he couldn't have Paul—"Fuck."

Justice barely missed the fist coming at his face. He grabbed Nischal's wrist and with a jerk, had the man in a hold that he wouldn't get out of without shifting.

"Cut it out, idiot," Justice snarled as Nischal jerked and squirmed. "I think he's my mate!"

Nischal stopped struggling. "What? Paul?"

The reality of those words, of the situation itself, hit Justice hard. He let go of Nischal. "Yeah. Yeah, I think so."

Nischal turned and glared at him. "You *think* so? How can you not know?"

Justice glanced towards the truck, where Preston and Paul were now sitting inside, their heads close together as they spoke.

"I never felt anything like I did even right before I saw him," Justice murmured, watching Paul and wishing he could touch him. "Everything inside of me came to life, and I never knew it had been dormant until then. When he looked at me, I couldn't do anything but follow him. Even now, after coming not ten minutes ago, I crave the chance to touch him, to—"

"I get it," Nischal said as he waved a hand at him. "Stop, okay?"

Justice did, glad that he was able to cut off the too-personal confession.

Nischal moved to stand beside him. "I'm guessing you're the guy whose sister is going to be Paul's therapist?"

"Justice Chalmers." Justice held out a hand to shake.

"Nischal. No last name." They shook and Nischal sighed. "Man, what a mess. Did you know who he was?"

Justice shook his head. "No. Not until Preston banged on the bathroom door. With the bleached hair, I didn't put it together."

"And the makeup. Paul's gone back to trying to cover up his freckles."

"He looks like your Preston?" Justice asked. "When he's not dying his hair and covering his skin?"

Nischal hitched a shoulder in a shrug. "Well, he does to a point. I can tell them apart, which is no surprise, considering Preston is my mate. Paul used to be a lot thinner, way too thin, but he's bulked up. Even more so since the last attack on him."

Justice cocked his head and told his leopard to calm the fuck down. There was no one to kill and punish for Paul's suffering just then. "Last attack?"

Nischal gave him a sideways look. "How much do you know about Paul? About what's happened to him?"

Crossing his arms over his chest, Justice contemplated the info he had. "I know he was kidnapped and sold into slavery in a human trafficking ring here in the US. There were shifters involved, wolf ones. I know he was hurt, probably very badly, and sexually abused." His stomach turned as he forced himself to continue. "I know now that what just happened between me and him was likely some need on his part to control his sexual needs, to—" He stopped.

Paul had touched him, there at the end. Now that he thought about it, there'd been something tentative in Paul's grip the first few strokes, then Paul had made a sweet, wanton sound as he'd tightened his hand around Justice's cock.

Nischal grunted and they stood there for another moment, two men in the middle of a parking lot that wasn't, thankfully, busy at that time. Still, they were lucky they hadn't been run over.

"You should go, get him back to Grandma's." Justice forced his gaze away from Paul. "He's going to hate me." Shifters had abused him. Justice couldn't imagine even a mate-bond getting Paul past that fact.

"I don't think so, but he will probably be pissed off." Nischal uncrossed his arms. "He was probably just as drawn to you as you were to him." He looked at Justice. "The desire for our mate is unfathomable to someone who has never experienced it. Once it hits, it controls us even as it demolishes our restraint. Paul won't be able to stay away."

"And he'll hate me for that," Justice whispered, aching at the knowledge of that truth. "This is going to make his life so much more difficult."

Nischal smacked him on the arm, hard enough to make Justice shuffle aside.

"What the fuck, asshole!"

Nischal wrinkled his nose at Justice. "Your grandma Marybeth is going to be twisting your ear and popping your nose a lot with that potty mouth you have."

Justice bit his lips and glared. Nischal was right, though.

"Anyway, that was for being a big emo dummy. You and Paul wouldn't be mates if it wasn't going to work. You two need each other. It just might take you both a while to figure it out. Have some faith in yourself." And with that, Nischal jogged over to the truck.

Justice turned away and went to his own vehicle. He was kind of glad he wasn't in the truck with Paul. When Nischal opened the door, raised voices spilt out. Justice hadn't heard them when he'd been speaking to Nischal, probably because he'd been so focused on himself and the conversation. Maybe, too, Paul and Preston hadn't been yelling then.

Justice wished he could revel in the joy of having found his mate, but it wasn't that simple. Maybe Nischal was right, and the Fates hadn't fucked up by pairing him with Paul. But it still wouldn't be easy. Paul had problems, justifiably so. Justice didn't want to do anything to make them worse.

Even then as he sat in his car contemplating what had happened in such a short period of time, Justice yearned for Paul. Not just sexually, though his dick was still trying to poke a hole in his jeans. No, he wanted to hold Paul, to comfort him and be there for him. To help him through the healing process.

He had a feeling that them being mates was going to test the mate bond in ways that might never have occurred before.

Justice thought about his cousins, many of whom had found their mate in the past couple of years. It was like once they knew about the possibility of it, they began finding that one special person. Not all of his cousins, of course, because damn, he had dozens of them. They were a large, prolific family. But still, it'd started with Levi, then several of the male cousins had got their happily ever after.

That was something Justice had thought about on occasion, but the closer he got to thirty, the more he'd dwelled on it. And moped, too, if he were honest. He'd come home from the military and missed the camaraderie of it. Ten years—it was all he knew, really, in his adult life. Then he'd moved back to Phoenix and got an apartment with Viv, determined to help her out in any way he could.

His friends were scattered all over the world, and he had lost touch with many of them. Only Asher and Tuck, his two best buds, were still on his contacts list. He was going to be a pathetic twit if he didn't watch out.

Justice shook himself like a cat doused with water. He wasn't a kid, and he'd lived a lot in his twenty-nine years. If he wanted to be what Paul needed, then he had better stop being a whiny shit and man the fuck up.

Viv would laugh at that and tell him if he was going to toughen up, he should woman the fuck up, but whatever. It was time that he put his best foot forward.

Chapter Five

Paul buried his head in his hands. "No!" There wasn't much else he could shout at Preston then, and even that was futile.

A shifter. A goddamned shifter! And I still want him, so much I want to jump out of the truck and chase him down! "Fuck!" Paul began rocking, the seatbelt cutting into him as he tried to calm his rising panic.

Except it wasn't just panic, and he hated to acknowledge that. Desire was burning in him, chasing away everything but the need to feel that big, hard body against his.

"He won't touch you again—" Preston began.

Nischal slammed his door. "Yeah, he will—"

"He won't!" Preston yelled, drowning out Nischal's voice. "I'll kill him if he tries!"

Paul's ears rang in the silence that followed that. Preston started the engine and Nischal remained silent, but Paul knew something had passed between them in that weird way they had of reading each other's mind. It was something that happened between destined mates, Preston had said.

It sounded like hell to Paul, having to share the darkness in his mind with someone else. He couldn't imagine being so exposed, or forcing the kind of shit he had upstairs onto someone else. If he cared for someone he sure as hell wouldn't want them seeing the poison in his soul.

But to know someone would be there for me, no matter what, like the couples I've seen at Marybeth's. Like Preston and Nischal…

It was unfathomable, and yet Paul yearned for it so much his eyes stung as tears threatened to fall. Paul pressed harder on his head then forced himself to uncurl. He was acting like a nut. It was no wonder Preston and everybody insisted he get help.

A shifter. I wanted – want, still – a shifter. God, I wanna touch him, lick him, do so many things to him. It wasn't freaking Paul out now that he had got past the initial panic. His dick was still hard, and there was a pleasant buzz of need humming through his veins.

It'd been so long since he'd felt anything like it. Paul closed his eyes and replayed the few short minutes he'd spent in the restroom with the man. He could still smell the earthy scent of his spunk. Shifter or no, Paul needed to see him again. He just hoped he didn't freak out and scare the guy off. Jesus, he hoped *he* didn't freak the fuck out, never mind the tall, built stranger losing it.

"Paul?"

Paul didn't bother opening his eyes. He didn't want to see pity directed his way. "Preston?" he replied, the way they used to play when they'd been kids.

Preston's chuckle sounded good to hear. Paul even smiled a little. "I'm okay," he even managed. Paul cupped his hands over his groin, hiding his erection. "Just tired."

"I—" Preston stopped to cough and Paul, knowing his brother as he did, waited for him to spit out whatever it was he wanted to say but feared Paul would hate hearing.

Preston barely held out for thirty seconds. "Justice is one of Marybeth's grandsons, so I know he isn't a dick. She wouldn't tolerate her kids or grandkids being anything less than honourable people. I've learnt that much in the time that Nisch and I have been staying there."

"You should see her go after Sabby," Nischal added, snickering. "I think he eggs her on just because he likes being scolded. Reminds him of our mama."

"As often as he's getting an ass-chewing, he must have been a big mama's boy then," Preston said wryly.

"He was. A kiss-up, always getting away with causing trouble." Nischal sighed. "I never could get away with anything, but that's okay. Mama loved me too."

"How could she not have?" Preston asked.

"If y'all get any sweeter I'm going to die from saccharine poisoning," Paul snarked, though really, he was glad for Preston.

"Is that even possible?"

Paul opened one eye to peek at his brother. "Too much of anything will kill ya." *Surely. Maybe.*

"Huh." Preston didn't sound convinced. "Well, if you say so. Anyway."

"Justice?" Paul said suddenly, the man's name registering. He sat up and opened both eyes. "His name is *Justice*? Who does that to a kid?"

Nischal turned around and frowned at him. "What's wrong with his name? It seems very honourable to me."

"Does he have siblings named Peace, Truth and American Way?"

Nischal's scowl darkened. "Don't be a jerk, Paul."

That Nischal was irked enough to get onto him knocked Paul back a step mentally. Nischal was either tired of his shit, or he thought Paul was capable of dealing with being scolded.

"One of his siblings is named Vivian," Nischal informed him. "Ring a bell?"

It did, instantly. Paul could feel his eyes bugging. "This is going to be fucking awkward." He was disappointed too, because for all his bitching about Preston insisting on getting him help, Paul had secretly been looking forward to it in a way. Hoping that it would do some good. Now… "Jesus, I can't sit with his sister! I had my—" He snapped his mouth shut so hard it hurt.

Nischal was still watching him, and the ass laughed, enjoying Paul's discomfort. Apparently Nischal was done pussy-footing around Paul. "Can I guess?"

"No!" Paul and Preston both shouted. Paul glowered at Nischal. "Pervert."

Nischal winked at him. "You're the one who mentioned it."

Paul turned his head and looked out of the window. He didn't see much more than a blur of green and blue. Preston had to be hauling ass. He closed his eyes again and vowed to stay quiet the rest of the ride. He'd worry about the weirdness of having Justice's sister as a therapist later on. For now, he wanted to savour the memory of the man's warm, skilled mouth sealing tight around his dick.

* * * *

Despite having been hungry earlier, Justice didn't bother hitting up the diner for food. His stomach was in knots and the urge to go after Paul was a battle he didn't know if he could resist much longer.

Doing the honourable thing, even when his instincts told him it wasn't, sucked. Everything in him wanted to find Paul and hold him, make him listen. But Paul had already been held against his will for a long time. Justice wouldn't do the same. He'd wait, and hope that Paul would come to him. They'd be close, anyway, both staying at Grandma Marybeth's.

Except he couldn't stay for more than a week. That was all the time he'd got off from work. Groaning, he thumped his head against the steering wheel. There was no way he could get off for longer, and he was certain Paul wasn't going to declare undying love and return to Phoenix.

Not yet, at least. Maybe not ever, if Paul was too damaged from his past—Justice sat up and shook his head. *No.* "No," he repeated out loud. "No, I won't give up on him. There's a reason we're mates, and my leopard is just going to have to pipe the fuck down if he doesn't want Paul scared off."

At the threat, his leopard did indeed pipe the fuck down, though there was some pathetic mewling, much like the human version of whining.

"We'll do our best, buddy, but Paul's health, mentally and physically, has to come first." Justice wasn't going to give up just because the road was likely to be rough. He wasn't a quitter.

He parked the car again and got out. A check of his phone showed the time to be a little before two. Hopefully Viv was done with her errands. He wanted to get their coming conversation over with as soon as possible, then get to Grandma's.

Justice texted Viv and got an almost instant reply. He headed over to the antique store, unsurprised to find his sister carrying several bags of stuff she'd bought. All but one of the bags bore the name of the boutique she'd gone to. The other one had the pharmacy's name on it.

"Let me have some of those." He took all of them since she shoved them at him.

"Thanks. Those bag are heavy as all get-out." She rubbed at the red marks on her right arm. "I was thinking about getting Grandma that lamp over there." She pointed at something that looked more like a piece of art than a lamp to him. Not the pretty art, either, but the fussy, pretentious, you'll-never-figure-out-what-it-is-because-you-aren't-smart-enough kind of art.

"Seriously?" he asked.

The sales clerk raised his head and glared at him. Justice shrugged. He hadn't even noticed the thin man standing behind the counter until then.

Viv only hummed and walked over to the lamp.

Justice followed her, trying not to knock anything over with the bags. Considering the crap in the store, and how cluttered the place was, that was probably the only way they made any sales.

"Viv, I really need to talk to you," he muttered as he got closer to her.

She stopped and pivoted around. She sniffed and he felt his blush on every inch of his skin. Viv planted a hand on one of her narrow hips. "Really, bub? I leave you alone for what, an hour, and you—" She looked around then lowered her voice. "Get laid? How does that even happen? I can't even get laid that easy and I'm an attractive woman!"

He winced, not wanting to think about his little sister and sex. *Not in this world.* She was going to remain a virgin in his mind forever just like his younger brothers. He didn't have a double standard for his siblings.

"Can I help you?"

The snootily asked question had him and Viv both sending startled looks towards the sales clerk.

"I'll take this lamp if you'll knock ten bucks off the price," Viv said, turning back to the ugly thing. "Grandma will love it."

"If you say so." Personally, Justice thought Marybeth would end up setting it on one of the coffee tables so either the dogs or a great-grandkid would knock it off and break it. That's what he'd do.

"It's a very high-quality piece of art," came that snotty voice again.

Justice rolled his eyes and sealed his lips shut. Telling the sales clerk it was fugly as hell would just be rude and confrontational. "I'll take these bags to the car then drive over and pick you up. And the lamp."

Justice edged his way out of the shop. The salesman turned his nose up and actually sniffed like some bad parody of a stuck-up jackass. The laughter slipped out of Justice before he could stop it. He rushed out of the door and kept chuckling almost all the way to the car.

Once he had everything loaded into the back seat, he got in and started the car. The seat belt buckle was hot from the sunlight. He snapped it in place and put the car in gear. As he drove down the street, he saw Viv step outside. The salesman was right beside her, holding that atrocious lamp.

As far as Justice could tell, the lamp was glass. Well, pieces of glass, and not in that pretty way that one company made lamps. This one kind of looked like someone had puked all over the place and the vomit had turned into glass. It was bile-green and shit-brown, and there were sparkly rhinestones and sequins on it. Maybe that was the name of the 'art' — Body Expulsions.

Grandma Marybeth was going to be surprised, that was for sure. Her decorating style was more country than…hell, he didn't even know what to call that lamp other than hideous.

He unfastened the seatbelt then got out to take the lamp and put it in the car, but the salesman huffed again and twisted away from him. "It's very delicate, not for the hands of brutes."

"What century do you think we're in?" Justice asked. "Brutes?"

"Imbecile."

"Well, all righty then." Justice couldn't help but grin at the puffed-up guy. A little flattery wouldn't hurt, though, because he hadn't meant to be a prick. "You do indignant really well. The red in your cheeks brings out the colour of your eyes."

"My eyes are brown, and red is hardly likely to change that in any way."

Justice gave up. Sometimes winning the battle meant taking away the ammunition, which in this case would be anything he said. He got back in the car and buckled up. The AC was just beginning to cool the car off and he wiped at the sweat on his brow.

Despite the potential problems, he was eager to get to Grandma Marybeth's. Hopefully he would see Paul again when they got there. Of course, there was always the very likely chance that Paul was going to hate him and hide from him.

Or... Maybe not. At least, maybe not for long. If the mate-bond works for us like it has for everyone else it's happened to, maybe Paul will be so drawn to me that he can't hate me. But would that fuck up his head?

"Would it?" Justice asked himself, letting the question sink in and grab him by the balls. He didn't want Paul to have worse problems because of him.

"Are you talking to yourself?" Viv asked as she opened the car door.

"Singing," he answered distractedly, trying to figure out whether him being Paul's mate could be a good thing for the man.

"You can't carry a tune in a bucket," Viv informed him as she sat and closed the door.

"Buckle up, brat." Justice didn't argue about his singing skills or lack thereof. His singing voice could peel the paint right off the walls.

"So what was so important that you had to talk to me immediately?" she asked him. "And why were you giving Clark a hard time?"

"Clark? Who the fuck is Clark?" Justice checked for traffic then pulled out onto Main.

"That very nice, and very gay, salesman back there." She smacked his arm. Damn, he was going to be bruised before the day ended. "Oh, wait, you don't care because you found someone to fuck already."

"Clark was a bit pompous for me." Which was being nice and generous on Justice's part. "And gross, sis. Don't talk about my sex life so blatantly."

"You reek of—"

"Stop!" he yelped before she could get any further. "I found my mate, okay?"

Viv leant forward and squealed. "You did? Where is he? Why isn't he here? Shouldn't you two be attached at the—"

"Viv," he warned.

"Hip?" she finished.

Justice exhaled and tapped the steering wheel as he drove. "I also met Paul." A side glance showed him Viv's frown.

"Paul? What does he have to do with your mate?" But before he could even answer, Viv smacked him again, hard. "He's your mate, and you had sex with him?"

"Stop screeching, and for fuck's sake, stop hitting me!" Justice snapped, shooting a glare at her. "Maybe you should check into your aggressive tendencies and do something about that."

Viv flipped him off. "You're my brother, and I'll smack you when you need it."

"I didn't know he was Paul when I followed him into the bathroom."

"Oh my God," Viv gasped. "You had a sleazy bathroom encounter? People really do that?"

"Viv, focus." He tried to organise his thoughts but gave up and just blurted it all out. "I stopped at the gas station." He gestured to it as they drove past. "Had to go the restroom, but as soon as I stepped inside the store, I felt—I don't know. Like everything inside of me was alive for the first time ever. I didn't know what the hell that meant." He wasn't going to mention the nearly instantaneous boner, either. "When I was heading to the restroom, this short, sexy guy stepped in front of me. He had bleached white-blond hair and green eyes."

"Bleached hair? Not orange?"

"Not orange," he confirmed. "Otherwise, maybe it would have clicked? I don't know. I was so bulldozed by lust that I wasn't even thinking." *Ew. I can't believe I just admitted that to my little sister!* "He looked back at me and I just knew he wanted me like I wanted him. So I followed him into the restroom."

"Did he use a condom?"

Justice glanced at her and realised she was taking notes on her phone. "What are you doing? Oh my God, are you taking notes on what I'm telling you? About my sex life?"

"About Paul's behaviour," she said only a little snarkily. "Get over your prudish self."

"I'm not a prude, it's just weird to have my sister writing down shit about stuff like that." He understood the why of it, however, so he quit bitching. "Yes, he put a condom on." Something occurred to him. "Wait, how'd you know he'd be putting on a condom?"

Viv clicked her tongue before answering. "I can't tell you that. It's confidential information."

Well, he wasn't stupid. If she knew Paul would have been wearing a condom, that was probably because his proclivity was to top and be in control. Understandable, considering the man's past. It also scared the fuck out of Justice. He'd dropped to his knees eagerly, but usually he was the one calling the shots—and he always topped. Could he bottom if Paul needed him to?

"It's good that he used a condom, though those things taste disgusting," Viv said.

"No." Justice shook his head. "No, you didn't just tell me you've—no, just no, Viv. Take that back!"

"Better be nice to me or I'll give you the details," she threatened. "How did Paul react? Did he touch you in return?"

"Viv, I am not going over what happened between us with you. I will say he didn't freak out. Neither of us spoke." Justice almost missed the turnoff for their grandma's place. He braked hard and turned onto the dirt and gravel road. "Then Preston began banging on the door, and he said Paul's name, and everything clicked. For me. Not for Paul. I think that happened later, when Preston thought he was rescuing Paul from me outside."

Justice told the rest of the story and Viv kept taking notes. They pulled into Grandma Marybeth's long driveway and Justice slowed the car down to a crawl. "Do you think what we did is going to make things worse for him?"

"I don't know," Viv said in her usual blunt manner. "Maybe, maybe not. The thing is, I don't know what it feels like to have a mate bond. From what I've heard, that bond should only help, not harm. It could be that you will offer a stability he really needs, but I'd hold off on the sex if you can. Let him initiate it, and if you can't do what he wants, then offer something else you can both agree on."

Justice clenched his butt. That sounded a lot like Viv was telling him Paul would want to top. "What about his fear of shifters?"

"He's here, isn't he?" Viv asked. "There are shifters all over the place. I think the main problem is with wolf shifters. They were the ones who hurt him."

Just hearing those words caused a wave of rage to roll over Justice. He had to take several deep breaths to fight it back down.

"Interesting," Viv crooned. Justice ignored her. He parked the car in the drive then unbuckled after turning the engine off.

"I'll get the bags and the lamp," he offered.

"Oh no you don't, I'll get the lamp. Don't be thinking you're getting any credit for this beauty." Viv touched the lamp.

"Not a problem. By all means, carry it." Justice grinned at her. "Just remember, ugly wears off. Don't handle it too much."

"Dick."

Chapter Six

Honestly, Paul couldn't figure out what was going on with him. His stupid dick wouldn't behave. It was like he had priapism or something. Except he thought he'd heard that was painful and he wasn't hurting. In fact, it felt good to be turned on. Truly turned on, horny, not seeking for release as a means to prove he was in control.

It was so strange. Paul blinked and pressed his forehead against the window. The cabin he was sharing with Preston and Nischal was new, and large. Good thing, considering Sabin lived there too. Paul wasn't quite sure what to make of Sabin. His white hair was a cause for envy. Paul could never get his hair that white. He bleached and toner'd it so much he was surprised it hadn't fallen out. It still had the faintest yellow tint to it.

Sabin didn't bother him. The first day or two, he'd tried being friendlier than Paul felt like dealing with. Paul had snapped and that had put an end to Sabin saying more than hi—maybe—to him.

Probably he should feel bad about that, but the fact was, Paul was tired, and so torn up inside he could hardly see past his own problems. It was a level of self-absorption that shamed him yet he couldn't shake it. His past had its claws so deeply entrenched in his psyche that he could hardly function like a normal person.

No, he *couldn't* function like a normal person.

He wished the cabin were closer to Marybeth's house. He'd like to see Justice—*Jesus, what a name*—again. The longing to do so had him twitching and putting his hands to the window, as if he could just seep through the glass and morph into a man on the other side of it.

Of course he could leave, go out of the door, but he'd have to walk past Preston and Nischal unless he went to the back door, and Sabin had been in the washroom last Paul saw, which meant he wouldn't get out unseen that way, either.

Or he could just tell them he was going to Marybeth's. There was a sudden tug in his gut that had him staring out of the window in that direction. Crazy as it seemed, he would have sworn that Justice had arrived. He couldn't know that, so maybe he was even crazier than he thought, because his mind was insisting the man was just a half mile away.

Paul curled his fingers against the glass. His cock throbbed as need coiled tighter in him. He wanted to touch Justice, to really touch him, to taste him, and one thing Paul did know about shifters, they didn't catch human diseases. Preston had even told him so.

Justice hadn't argued about the condom, though. Did that mean Justice had been so desperate for him that he'd acquiesced to the use of latex?

Paul remembered the need in those pretty eyes. Justice had looked up at him and Paul had seen the raw lust there. It had shaken him to his core, because he'd felt the same thing. Still felt it as he stood at the window.

He heard a throat cleared behind him and knew it was Preston. One glance in the window showed him his twin's reflection.

"Are you okay?" Preston asked.

Paul almost reverted to that sickening self-pity he'd been rolling around in. It took him a minute to work past it. He turned enough to prop his shoulder on the window frame and look at his brother, but he kept one hand dangling—casually, he hoped—over his erection.

"I will be, maybe, one day." Paul shrugged his other shoulder. "Today, I'm still a mess. I feel…" He searched for a way to explain it then shook his head. "I don't know. I can see that I spent months taking dangerous risks that were contrary to me saying I wanted to live. I don't know why." That wasn't the crux of his problems just then, but he wasn't sure he wanted to talk about Justice with Preston.

His brother knew him like no one else did, at least when it came to some things. Preston cocked his head. "What about Justice?"

"I want justice," Paul answered, "Who wouldn't? What was done to me was wrong."

Preston gave a much-put-upon sounding sigh and rolled his eyes. "I meant, the man Justice, but yeah, of course you want the other kind. I hope I get to beat the shit out of some of those assholes, Paul. I've never wanted to kill anyone before, but God, do I want to now."

Paul looked away. He hated that his brother felt such hatred. It wasn't his fault, he knew that on some level, but he couldn't make it sink in. If he hadn't been stupid enough to go to the sideshow featuring the snow leopards, if he hadn't flirted with the man hosting the damned show then, if he hadn't been fucking stupid—

"I really think you need to talk to Justice," Preston said, cutting through Paul's thoughts. "I don't know about the sex part of it, but I doubt you'll be able to avoid him here."

"Why do you think I need to talk to him?" Paul asked as his heart fluttered at the thought of it. "Please don't dwell on my sex life."

"But—" Preston began. Paul held up one hand.

"No." Okay, that kind of wasn't fair and he knew it. Paul sighed internally. "Look, I told you about what I was doing, and that I figured out, finally, that it wasn't about sex. It wasn't. Today, with Justice? It was definitely about sex. Sex, and need, and…" To Paul's utter humiliation, tears pooled in his eyes and spilt over in a heartbeat. "Shit!" He swiped at them and averted his face. He didn't want to be such a pathetic twit. "Don't," he rasped when he heard Preston approaching. If Preston hugged him, he just might shatter.

"Paul." Preston sounded as gutted as Paul felt.

Paul scrubbed at his face until his skin burned. "I just felt good for a few minutes today. Imagine that, feeling like a god in a dingy bathroom at a truck stop."

Preston laughed, the sound coming across as rather forced. "I bet lots of guys can say that, actually. How many stories have you heard about hook-ups at rest stops and restrooms?"

"Dark alleys and dance floors, bathhouses." Paul grinned at his brother, some of his funky mood fading. "I even saw this video of two guys fucking in a lumber store. That one was wild but boring, too."

Preston bobbed his head. "Oh my God, I know what you mean. I saw it too. They couldn't move much or make any noise, so the sex itself wasn't all that, but the idea of them doing it in public was kinda hot. Until I thought about some poor little kid running around a corner and getting an eyeful."

"Or someone getting a handful later on when they grabbed a two-by-four," Paul said.

He and Preston snickered like they'd reverted to their teenage years. It felt good—so twice in one day, Paul had come up out of the darkness that seemed to swamp him constantly. Maybe there really was hope for him yet. It'd be nice if he could keep those promises of getting better. God knew Preston had been through enough looking for him.

After a minute or two, Preston came closer and hooked an arm around Paul's waist. "Seriously, maybe you and Justice should talk."

Paul tipped his head to the side and studied his brother. "Are you playing matchmaker? You seem to think that a hookup in the restroom might mean eternal love."

Preston jerked his gaze away, denying Paul a chance to read those windows to his soul. "No, but I think you've had a hard-on all this time, and maybe that's something, and you said you felt good with him for a few minutes, so that's another something. And you laughed with me, Paul. I've waited for that for so long."

What was he scared of? He wanted to see Justice, and do every raunchy thing with him that he could think up. All those nights he'd been out fucking around, he hadn't wanted to touch whoever he was with. This was so different. He didn't just want it with Justice, he was beginning to think he needed it.

"Marybeth will be sticking her nose into it if I show up, especially since I haven't showered," Paul pointed out. "Give me about ten minutes, okay?"

"Okay," Preston agreed. "Although she has a sharper scenting ability than Nischal, so unless Justice has showered, there's a damn good chance Marybeth will know whose scent is on him."

"Shit." Paul was glad he wasn't in Justice's shoes right now, not if the old lady was pissed about him hooking up with Paul.

Then again, she might not give a damn. Paul was just a human, the brother of one of her long-lost relatives' mate.

"That's not confusing at all," Paul mumbled as Preston left the room. Paul left his spot by the window and headed for the bathroom. He had some serious scrubbing to do.

* * * *

Justice covered his sore ear. "Grandma, I didn't know!" Gods, being a shifter had its downsides, especially if your grandma was also a shifter and she smelt sex and Paul on you. Then you were just fucked.

"That's the only reason I didn't twist your ear plumb off," Grandma Marybeth told him. "Although since you let your sister buy that god-awful lamp and give it to me…"

Justice danced back a few steps. "You told her—"

"Hush, boy, she's coming back." Marybeth patted her hair then looked at her nails. "The lamp will be lovely on the end table by the door."

Right where it could easily be knocked off. Justice would bet the lamp would be broken in under a month. Probably right after he left.

"Oh, Grandma, that's not a good spot. It'll get broken in no time," Viv said as she came back into the room. "Your bathroom sink is dripping, too. Justice can fix it if you want."

"No, that's not his job," Marybeth said, flapping a hand at Viv. "Oscar has already promised to fix it this evening. He'll be mad if someone beats him to it."

Justice arched a brow at his grandma. "Well, if that was supposed to dissuade me from fixing it…"

She pointed a finger at him. "Don't get your cousin wound up. It wasn't all that long ago that Oscar had you pinned to the ground, calling Uncle."

"Nope, and I owe him for that," Justice informed her as he edged towards the hallway. "Think he'll want to wrestle me again? It's been a year and a half."

"Because you missed the last family reunion," Marybeth groused. "Oscar had to wrestle Marvin instead."

Laughter slipped from his lips at that. "Marvin? Uncle Marvin? He has to be seventy!"

Marybeth sent him a searing look. "Marvin is younger than I am."

"Yes, ma'am." He wasn't totally stupid. "You know why I couldn't be here for the family reunion. There was nothing I could do about it."

"Leave the sink alone and go answer the door instead," was all she told him.

Justice wondered how long his grandma was going to give him shit for missing the reunion. It wasn't like he could skip out on the mandatory training he'd had to attend. Being a Phoenix policeman had been a dream of his as a boy. He'd joined the military first, though, just to give it a try. Being a cop was a better fit in the long run.

He hadn't heard anyone pull up. Justice frowned just as a knock sounded. How had his grandma known someone was coming?

Justice grabbed the door knob and a sense of déjà vu hit him. He suddenly saw himself standing at the door, reaching for the knob, turning it, all as if he were an observer from a distance rather than the man doing it. The weird sensation stopped when he began to pull the door open.

Then he was looking at Paul. Someone else was beside Paul, but Justice didn't particularly care who it was. All he could see were those sexy green eyes, and the wary look on Paul's face.

Wary. That was a kick in the balls. Justice pushed at the screen door while stepping back as far as he could. "Come in." Damn, his voice had gone all husky on him.

"Thanks." That wasn't Paul. Justice finally looked to the other man.

"Preston." He nodded. Preston did the same. "Grandma is in the den. Watch out for the ugly lamp. She loves that thing and will be upset if it gets broken." If Marybeth was going to give him shit, he was going to dole a little bit of it right back to her. Maybe she'd have that lamp longer than she planned on it.

Preston hooked his arm through Paul's but Paul grunted and tapped his brother's hand. "I'm fine. Go on."

Paul was fine? Justice looked him over, taking his time. Paul was short, compact, and now, without the makeup on, Justice could see the numerous freckles on his face and neck.

He wanted to kiss each one.

Paul's eyelashes were thick and dark where they met skin, but the tips were gold, and looked soft as down. His eyebrows held a high arch, either by design or nature. Paul's lips were plump but not outrageously so. The pale mauve colour of them reminded Justice of a pomegranate sorbet he'd had once at a fancy restaurant in Phoenix. It'd been sweet and cool, just like he imagined Paul's lips would be.

He realised they were standing there and that he was ogling Paul. Justice bit back a curse and stepped out onto the porch. Paul followed him, pulling the door shut behind them.

"I didn't know it was you," Justice said, turning to face Paul. He looked at that bleached hair. "I guess I expected hair like Preston's. You had your freckles covered up, too." He wondered if Paul's hair was soft or pokey, like Viv's had been after she'd dyed it three times in one day. Her hair had been as brittle as thin strands of spun glass.

"I hate these freckles," Paul muttered. "The orange hair and them, Jesus, you have no idea how many times they've caused me trauma."

Justice imagined Paul wasn't just talking about teasing.

"I wasn't allowed to cut my hair, you know." Paul glanced at him, checking, Justice thought, to see if he knew what Paul was talking about. Justice nodded slightly and Paul's entire face turned red as he looked away. "Yeah, figured you knew. They liked my hair and freckles, just as much as I hate them."

Justice had no idea what to say. From his understanding, mates were able to develop a mental bond, but he wasn't feeling any of that with Paul. *Maybe it just takes time, or he probably has up some massive walls, considering.*

"I like the blond." Justice shrugged, even though Paul wasn't looking at him. The fact was, he'd like Paul with any colour of hair, or none at all. And he loved the freckles—they'd always driven him nuts on a lover.

"Why?" Paul did look at him then, a shuttered expression that Justice couldn't read. "I mean, why did you follow me today? Do you do stuff like that often?"

Translation—was I just an easy piece of ass? Justice turned to face Paul fully. He looked him over from head to toe, noting the erection that matched his own. Every bit of Paul's exposed skin right down to his fingertips was blushing. Justice met Paul's gaze.

"No, I don't. I'm not saying I haven't ever had a one-night stand, but I saw you and something inside of me recognised you." He watched Paul start to fidget, knew he was trying not to ask the question on the tip of his tongue. Paul finally asked anyway.

"Why? I'm nothing special. If you'd have known who I was—"

"I'd still have followed you," Justice admitted, "But I'd have tried to talk to you instead of sucking you off in the restroom." He slowly reached for Paul's arm, just needing to touch the man briefly. He wanted more, but he would settle for the quickest touch to that soft skin.

And it was soft, and warm. Justice brushed his fingers over the ridge of muscle and Paul shivered.

"You are special, Paul. You have people here who care about you."

"Preston," Paul said, then he sucked on his bottom lip.

Justice nearly came on the spot. *Down, warped libido!* Now wasn't the time or place. "Marybeth, and I bet Nischal too. Mates are very close. They share almost every feeling." He swallowed as Paul's lip was released. It glistened and was darker from being bitten. "Mates need each other. It's a craving, an urge that lies dormant until the two meet, then it comes to life and demands the two touch, talk."

Justice moved an inch closer. So did Paul as he looked up at Justice with big, hope-filled eyes. "They do?" Paul asked.

Justice nodded and caressed Paul's arm again. "They do. I'm sure you've seen the way your brother and Nischal can't seem to be apart. It's hard on mates, or so I've heard. They want to be with each other. Sometimes, I guess, they can't, not right away." Gods, he didn't even know what he was trying to say. He just kept rambling as Paul inched ever closer.

"I'm a mess," Paul uttered. His eyes were streaked with red, as if he were battling back tears. "You're the first person I've touched like that since—" He broke off and started to move away.

Justice cupped his elbows. "Please." He waited, not holding Paul, just touching him. "You don't have to tell me anything. Just don't leave yet."

Paul trembled, but after a moment, he raised his eyes to Justice's. "I hope your sister can help me."

"She can," Justice asserted. "More importantly, you can help yourself. You want things to be different, you recognise the necessity for it."

Paul bobbed his head. "I do. I can't keep going on like I was." Then he edged closer. "They found me, two of the wolf shifters, in Denver. That's when I broke down, after some other guy stepped in and attacked them. I just lost it when I got home. I don't even remember—" He shook his head and took another half-step towards Justice. "I was so scared, and I couldn't breathe. Then Preston was there. I might be crazy."

"No, you're not." Justice brought a hand up to run his fingers along Paul's jaw. There was a hint of prickly stubble that shone golden under the sunlight. "Isn't there a saying about crazy people not thinking they're crazy?"

Paul's smile was slight but beautiful to see. "So I'm not insane because I think I am? Somehow that makes less sense to me."

Justice found the fluttery spot on Paul's neck where his pulse was racing. "I'm a cop in Phoenix. I've seen crazy, and believe me, you're not it."

"A cop?" Paul's eyes looked positively huge. "You're a cop?"

"Only recently," Justice told him. "I was in the Marines for a decade, then I applied to the Phoenix PD. I'd managed to get a degree online over the years, which helped. That, and being a vet." He chuckled. "Man, I thought Grandma was going to fly out to Phoenix and rip everyone at the training academy a new one because I was going to miss the annual family reunion."

"Marybeth is something," Paul said. "What's happening? Between us?" Paul clarified. His face turned an even brighter shade of red. "I mean, something is, right? I can't understand why you're touching me, or talking to me—"

"Your self-esteem needs some lifting, because you should know you're one gorgeous fucker, Paul." Justice traced Paul's lips with his thumb. "Your eyes—damn, you could ask me for anything, to do anything, and I'd do it just because you looked at me like you're doing now."

"I don't understand this," Paul muttered, lowering his lids but still watching him. "I haven't been able to let another man touch me since I was freed, and yet I want to snuggle right in." His sharp bark of laughter showed his surprise at either his admission or the urge itself. "Oh damn, I can't believe I just said that."

Which answered Justice's question. "Paul." Justice eased him closer but didn't embrace him. He wanted to shout for joy when Paul tentatively put a hand on his hip. Justice took a deep breath, inhaling Paul's soap and citrus scent. The man smelt delectable. "We're mates," Justice said as he exhaled, keeping the words as soft as his heart when it came to Paul. Already Justice knew he'd give the man anything. That in itself was proof to him of what they were to each other.

Paul jerked his head back and those eyes went wide again. Instead of red, though, he went pale as a ghost. "M-mates? No, we can't be."

That didn't sound good at all. Justice didn't stop Paul from moving away from him this time. Paul was shaking his head, staring with those wide eyes, hope still in them though Paul seemed to be trying to deny it.

"I'm too messed up. Look at today. I just wanted to get off—"

"And you touched me, like you haven't anyone else," Justice continued when Paul stopped to take a breath. "You let me touch you, too, up until you scooted away. Is it so horrible, the idea of us being mates?"

Paul backed up another step and stared at him. Justice was about to give up on him answering when Paul finally spoke again. "Not for me, no, but for you? Come on, Justice. How am I supposed to think you'd be happy about being stuck with me? Do you have any idea how many men have fucked me? What they've done to my body, my head?"

The anger in Paul's voice matched the anger flaring inside Justice, but he kept it buried. It wouldn't help Paul right then. "I wish they hadn't hurt you, Paul, but they did, and I can't change that. All I can do is tell you it doesn't—it won't—stop the way I'll feel about you. It won't stop you from wanting me, either. The mate-bond is very strong. I'd always heard it was so, but feeling it..." He pressed a hand to his belly, where need was uncoiling and spreading to his groin.

Paul nodded, glancing down at his hand, then lower still to where Justice's dick pressed against the inseam of his jeans. "Right, but you're getting the short end of the stick in the deal. There's... I can't even—fuck. I can't talk about this!"

It was a dismissal, Justice supposed. He didn't want to leave Paul, but at least he'd got to see him, hear him, touch him. He'd said what needed to be said, because keeping what they were to one another from Paul would have been wrong. Justice wanted to hold him, to soothe him with touches and kisses, but couldn't, and it made his heart ache.

"I understand." Justice took a step back himself. "Look, I think Grandma is putting us in one of the new cabins. I won't be very far from you if you need to talk, or want to. Or want anything. I'll leave it in your hands, no pressure." Gods, it was such a difficult thing to say and mean, but Justice wouldn't push. "Go on in, meet Viv and maybe you'll be able to talk to her. I'm going to go stretch my legs."

Paul shuddered. "You mean shift and run?"

"I do," Justice agreed. "I can't change what I am, Paul. All I can promise you is, I'm not like the shifters who hurt you. I hope you'll believe that someday." If not, Justice was going to be a miserable son of a bitch. He had to have faith in the bond that was coming to life between them, though. Had to trust the Fates. Justice tipped his chin at his mate, then turned and strode down the porch. Maybe he'd find some kind of solace under the sun, with the wind ruffling his fur.

It was difficult not to look back, but Justice didn't. Paul needed time to think about what Justice had told him. Standing anywhere near to each other wasn't helping, not when part of Justice could only think about having Paul's hands on him. If Paul was feeling even a smidgen of the lust Justice was, thinking was impaired.

Justice stripped his clothes and shoes off after he rounded the third cabin. Whoever was living in it wouldn't freak out if they saw him. He thought it was Oscar and his mate Josiah. That gave him pause. Josiah was a wolf shifter. How would having Josiah around affect Paul?

That was something Justice would have to talk over with Marybeth, and Viv, and maybe Paul if he could. Right now, though, he needed a break from thinking. His leopard was restless, frustrated—randy as hell and wanting to mate, but it wasn't going to happen. Justice knelt and closed his eyes as the shift came over him. It wasn't exactly fun, all the popping tendons and constricting muscles. In fact, it hurt like a fucking bitch, but that was part and parcel of being a snow leopard shifter. He'd heard something about some of his cousins figuring a way around the pain. That was another thing he needed to talk to his grandma about.

Later. Justice opened his eyes to a sharper world. Everything was brighter, louder, smellier, and not all in a bad way. He loved the way his senses were so finely honed as a snow leopard. Someday, he wanted to spend a week or so in a cold, snowy climate. It was probably weird that a snow leopard shifter lived somewhere as hot as Phoenix, but he was also a man who wanted to be near his family, so the heat was something he had to deal with.

But to be able to run through mounds of snow...that would sure be something.

Something he'd dream about and maybe someday experience. Justice let the longing go and bounded into the forest, ready to give his leopard its head.

Chapter Seven

Vivian Chalmers looked so much like her brother it was almost unreal. *Except for the boobs.* Those were something Justice didn't have, though his tight T-shirt had emphasised his well-defined pecs.

"Is this going to be too awkward for you?" Vivian asked Paul. "If it is, I understand."

Paul hitched a shoulder in a shrug. "I honestly don't know."

Vivian leant back in the chair. They were seated in the living room of the cabin Paul had been staying in. He had to admit, it did make him more comfortable, made him feel almost safe to be there.

"I'd like to suggest that we refrain from talking about my brother while we're in sessions," Vivian said. "Unless it's in context with what we're dealing with, of course."

"He told me we're mates," Paul blurted out.

Vivian hummed and seemed to give the barest nod. "Yes, and that might be problematic. You told me in your last email what some of your perceived issues were."

"Perceived?" Paul repeated, feeling his eyebrows crawl up his forehead. "They aren't perceived, they're real. I mean, I'm not the brightest paint chip in the rainbow, but even I know that I had been taking risks that could have led to my death. Then there's the whole thing where I have some fucked-up sexual hang-ups now and was just shoving my dick into any willing man I could find, as long as he'd let me have it my way. I didn't even enjoy the sex!" he all but shouted, frustrated and wanting Justice despite everything colliding about in his head. "It was all about control!"

"You hadn't had any control over you or your body in over a year, Paul. I think reclaiming some of that control was necessary for your psyche, but the risk-taking, that is worrisome." Vivian tapped a finger against her chin as she glanced out of the window. After a few seconds she looked at him again. "What do you think your reason for engaging in risky behaviour was?"

What did he think it was? "Isn't it your job to tell me?" God, he was being a bitch.

Vivian didn't seem the least bit fazed. "I firmly believe the most gripping, and lasting, revelations, come from the person seeking them."

"Well, fuck," Paul huffed. He ran a hand over his short hair. It made him feel kind of nauseated to parse out the reasoning behind his actions, but it came down to one thing, didn't it? "I guess I thought I was so fucked up, it didn't matter if I died. That'd be easier than trying to fix myself and trying to overcome my past. I couldn't just kill myself, though. Preston would have been devastated. If someone killed me, that'd be different. Easier, like he wouldn't feel like he'd failed me."

"You honestly think he wouldn't feel that way?"

"No," Paul answered unhesitatingly. "He'd have felt like shit regardless. I was being a coward. I was stupid. I just—it's like something inside of me was broken. I don't know if it can ever be pieced together again."

Paul pulled his legs up onto the couch and tucked his arms around his knees as he continued talking, the words just spilling out of him. "You have to understand, I was tortured, raped, treated like I was nothing. Oh, I was cared for, too, because no one wants a completely broken toy. I was patched up after they hurt me. I'd had more stitches than Frankenstein by the time I was rescued. The outside, though, that shit is healed. I can't…" Paul's chest tightened and his throat closed up. His next breath was a wheeze.

"Paul, listen to me. Try to calm down. Whatever you're thinking about, push past it and focus on something good, something that doesn't frighten you. Take slow breaths, because the more you pant, the less you feel like you're getting air. *Breathe.*"

Vivian's words penetrated his building panic in fits and starts. Paul tried, letting go of his legs and bending. A hand on his back helped, pushing his head down between his knees.

Paul drew in a deep breath even though his mind was racing, telling him he wasn't getting air. Images tangled in his mind, teeth and claws, cocks and pain.

Then something else penetrated his nightmarish memories. It started as a remembered touch, someone who wanted only to comfort him, not hurt him. Other things were added—a deep, soothing voice, the scent of woods and sage, eyes that looked upon him with kindness, not pity or hatred.

He wanted Justice there. Paul dragged in another breath, dizzy from the panic attack that had slammed into him. Vivian was still talking in a low, soft voice, but Paul didn't pay attention to the words. What he realised was that she had her hand on his back, and it felt so good to have someone touch him without wanting anything from him. Without wanting to hurt him.

Paul gasped but quickly forced himself to return to his attempts at slow-breathing. Preston was scared to touch him, Paul saw it in his eyes. Nischal wasn't close enough to him, and Sabin probably thought Paul was one fucked-up bitch, which was true enough. Marybeth and the other shifters walked on eggshells around him. Hell, some had even left the family home, like Oscar and his mate.

Marybeth had said they were due for a visit with Josiah's family, but Paul wasn't a fool. The only people there were Marybeth, Preston, Nischal and Sabin.

And now, Justice and Vivian. Paul's chest didn't feel so tight when he thought about Justice. Even through his panic, desire was building. He concentrated on Justice, letting himself focus only on him. Paul kept it clean, not drifting into thoughts of sex, instead wrapping himself in an imaginary embrace by the man. He could almost feel Justice sitting behind him, his inner thighs against Paul's outer, Justice surrounding him, his chest to Paul's back and those muscled arms running the length of Paul's own.

Justice would hold him, let Paul borrow some of that strength. A man who'd served ten years in the Marines, and was now a cop, had to have an inner core of steel. Surely Paul could draw from that, with them being mates and all.

* * * *

Halfway up a mountain, the panic slammed into Justice. He yowled and stumbled as his nervous system went haywire. Breathing became damn near impossible. Fear swamped him thoroughly, hazing his vision.

Justice tried to shake it off, like a physical attacker. He shook from nose to the tip of his tail. The feelings didn't fling off like water, though, and he dropped to his belly, his mind abuzz with more chaos than he could handle.

There were images bursting into his brain. Disturbing, horrific ones that made him growl and snarl as he pawed at the ground. He knew then what was happening. That mental bond he'd longed for had somehow opened, and Paul's hellish memories were rushing through it.

Paul must have been in session—Gods, Justice hoped he was in session with Viv, otherwise, who would help Paul through this?

I will, I so fucking will. If he was getting mental images and thoughts from Paul, then Paul should be able to get some from him. The difficult part would be getting past all the horror crowding Paul's brain.

It was jarring, and fucking terrifying for Justice. He'd had doubts over things he'd done here and there—who didn't? But this was self-doubt on a whole new level, and it'd been ripped and pounded into Paul by vengeful, sadistic shifters. It wasn't Paul's own doing, but the casual disregard for him as a human being at all, by the hands of others.

He'd been reduced to a thing, to be used and degraded, ignored then fawned over just to build his hopes. Only to have them crushed in ways so vile Justice ended up retching.

Even as he did so, he willed soothing thoughts to his mate, nothing concrete, just calmness, acceptance, affection. Justice wanted to give him so much more, but that would come with time. At that moment, he gave what he could.

And Paul took it, soaking it in like a dry sponge doused with water. Paul's need wrapped around him, and together they worked towards calming their bodies down.

When the panic eased to be replaced with gratitude, Justice mewled and rolled over onto his back. He rolled his neck and let the sun warm his belly and chase away the lingering chill left behind from that sudden assault of fear.

Paul would possibly feel guilty and regret reaching out to him, but Justice wouldn't let him sink under that weight. He kept sharing his own contentedness. Gods knew there wasn't anything else like lying there sunning himself. His leopard might be a creature originally born to snowy climates, but it sure as hell loved warming up under golden rays.

Justice purred and stretched his front legs, pawing at the air. He swished his thick, furry tail back and forth, sending dirt and rocks scattering about. The ground wasn't soft beneath him, but his coat was dense enough to make it all just fine and comfortable. The only thing missing was having his mate nearby, but that day would come. Justice doubted Paul would be eager to see him in shifted form.

His leopard mewled piteously over that, but he reassured the beast that the time would come when all of him was welcomed by Paul. They just needed to be patient, and let Paul lead.

Justice managed to doze for a while, peace flowing between him and his mate. He hoped Paul was doing the same, curled up somewhere warm and safe, thinking of him.

Birds chirped and squirrels chattered. They'd all been silent before, hiding from the predator that Justice was. He guessed they either thought he was dead or asleep and harmless. Birds and squirrels weren't his preferred meals anyway, but he couldn't tell them that. Now, give him a nice, healthy deer, or a fat bunny, and he was one happy cat.

His tummy rumbled and Justice pried an eye open. Judging by the sun's position, he'd probably been lazing about for an hour or so. He stretched, then did it again because it felt almost as good as getting off at that moment. Rolling onto his stomach, he raised his head and opened his other eye, too.

The sky was such a bright blue it almost made his eyes ache. There wasn't a cloud to be seen. A hawk soared high overhead. If Justice could have any one special ability—other than his shifter one—he'd love to be able to fly. He imagined there was a freedom to it that nothing else could match.

Justice came to his feet and stretched again, arching his back and sticking his butt up to really get his spine feeling good. Then he loped up the mountain, even though he wanted to go down and run to his mate.

He had to let Paul come to him. That wasn't possible right now, what with Justice a couple of hours' worth of running away from the cabin. Paul needed to rest, and Justice thought that might be what he was doing. There was nothing coming from that newly opened link between them but a steady hum of what he could only describe as white noise.

Justice didn't go all the way up the mountain. He'd save that for another time. He just went up to find the buck he'd been stalking earlier. His leopard was eager to take down the deer, but when it looked up at him, something stopped Justice. He saw the fear, and the will to live in the animal's eyes.

When the buck took off, Justice and his leopard had a battle of wills. By the time it was over, the deer was gone and Justice's leopard was pouting.

Yeah, he guessed it'd been stupid to hold back. He was a predator, at least part of him was, and denying that was foolish. He put his hesitation down to his experience with Paul earlier. Having seen some of the violence the man had been a victim of had put Justice off hurting anything else. He'd have to get past it, but for today, he'd let it go. He turned and began the trip back to the cabin, and hoped Viv had something cooked for dinner when he got there, or maybe Marybeth had fixed her awesome pot roast.

If not, he was capable of making something. Peanut butter sandwiches would work. Hell, he might just lick the peanut butter right out of the jar. The cabin would be stocked, that much Justice knew. No grandma, and especially not his grandma, would risk their grandkids being hungry.

Two and a half hours later, he was pleasantly worn out from the long run. He shifted and walked out of the trees, only to stop like he'd hit a glass wall.

Paul was sitting on the grass, staring at him hungrily. He had a blade of grass between his fingers, as if he'd been perusing it. Paul dropped it as he pushed himself up to his feet. His gaze raked over Justice repeatedly, studying him from top to bottom.

There was nothing Justice could do to keep his dick from filling. The instinct to breed was as ingrained as breathing. He could, however, keep from reaching for Paul.

But he looked Paul over just as thoroughly. Paul was a good six inches or so shorter than he was. His white-blond hair looked damp, as if he'd just showered. Justice inhaled and smelt soap mixed with orange and lemon. The tangy scent of it made his mouth water.

Paul's eyes seemed a darker green and he realised it was because Paul's pupils had dilated, chasing out all but a thin ring of the irises. There were pink stripes on Paul's cheeks, signs of arousal. His nostrils flared with every indrawn breath. His lips were pressed tightly together, compressing their fullness into a thin pink line.

The corded tendons in his neck stood out, a sign of him restraining himself. His shoulders were broader than Preston's, muscled thickly, just as his arms and chest were.

Justice could easily make out the prick of Paul's nipples beneath his cotton button-up. Paul was wearing those faded jeans that looked butter-soft and fit him like a glove. His cock pushed against the material and a damp spot appeared as Justice watched. Paul's thighs tensed, the muscles rippling.

Paul's voice startled Justice. "Can I…can I t-touch you?"

But not as much as that request.

Justice was so afraid of screwing up that he didn't reply verbally, instead nodding. Paul gulped and squeezed his left wrist. He looked so needy, so torn and unsure. Justice knelt, hoping that if he did so, his greater height wouldn't seem imposing. He canted his head to the side, a move that Paul might recognise as a sign of submission. Sweat slicked Justice's skin as he waited, watching Paul rub his wrist until the skin was dark red. He'd just about conceded defeat when Paul took a tentative step forward.

Paul's second step was quicker, as was his third and fourth. When he stopped in front of Justice a dozen steps later, he'd stopped trying to twist his wrist off. His hands were shaking, but then again, all of him was. Justice would have caressed those shakes away if he'd thought Paul would let him.

As it was, he lowered his gaze and stared at Paul's bare feet. He had elegant toes, something Justice had never understood before when he heard other people say it or when he'd read it in a book. But it was true. Paul's feet were pretty, pale and dotted with honey-coloured freckles.

From the corner of his eyes, he saw Paul reach for him at the same time he heard Paul inhale sharply. Justice had to close his eyes as Paul touched his cheek. Paul didn't stroke, only held his palm against Justice's face. Justice canted his head and rubbed his cheek over Paul's hand, unable not to.

Something close to a sob escaped from Paul. Justice snapped his eyes open and was going to tell Paul it was okay, but he didn't get the chance. Paul grabbed him at the nape and kissed him with a brutal force that was still erotic. It wasn't anger that was fuelling Paul's assertiveness, but a need that flowed into Justice.

Justice could and would meet that need. He could allow Paul to have him in any way necessary. Anything, anyway, Paul wanted. Justice kept his body relaxed as he allowed his head to be tipped back and his mouth to be plundered. Paul whimpered and bit at his lips, stinging nips that might have broken skin. Justice didn't care. His leopard was a rough son of a bitch who enjoyed the way he was being manhandled just as much, to his surprise, as Justice did.

Paul shoved and Justice went over backwards. Paul went right down on top of him, not letting up on the kiss. Their teeth clacked together when Justice hit the ground.

Paul lifted his head. "Oh God," he rasped, regret pinching his features. "I'm sorry! I—you're bleeding."

Justice did move then, framing Paul's face with his hands and leaning up, straining for more kisses. He rumbled happily when Paul gave him what he needed, diving back into the kiss like it'd never been interrupted.

Paul's hands were all over him, fleeting touches that spurred Justice's desire higher and higher. Paul hadn't touched any of the usual erotic spots yet, either, and Justice was dangerously close to coming already.

It was Paul's need, his hunger, that was driving Justice to the edge. Paul straddled his waist and ground forward and down, rubbing his denim-covered cock against Justice's belly. He wanted to touch Paul all over, but the thought was in his mind that he might still scare Paul off, so Justice kept his hands framing Paul's sweet face.

Paul kept kissing him, plunging his tongue deep in time with the thrust of his shaft against Justice's stomach. It was difficult not to shove his hips up and get some friction for his dick, but knowing Paul's past, Justice wouldn't make any such move.

He rubbed his palms over Paul's jaws as Paul nipped and sucked at his bottom lip. Paul rutted harder, faster, then he grunted and dragged his mouth over Justice's cheek. He kept scraping over skin, down Justice's neck to the spot where shoulder and neck joined. The instant Paul bit, hard, painfully so, Paul's muffled shout was countered by Justice's much louder one. Spunk warmed Justice's stomach through the material of Paul's jeans as Paul sucked the wound and rocked against him.

Then Paul was wiggling, moving, and a hand was on Justice's dick, jerking him off with harsh quick strokes. Paul left off biting his neck to move down and teeth one of Justice's nipples.

Justice bucked and yelped, pain and pleasure colliding in him in an exquisite dance. He lasted one more stroke, one more bite, then he was coming so hard his head spun.

He was out of it for a few minutes, he thought, but came to with Paul's panicked, "Oh my God, what did I do?" in his ear.

Justice opened eyes he'd apparently closed at some point. He had a nauseating second where he thought his mate was regretting the intimacy between them before he realised Paul was staring in horror at the spot where he'd bit Justice's neck.

Justice touched the spot. It was damp, and his fingers came back bloody. Paul looked absolutely horrified. Justice wasn't having that. He sat up and grinned cockily.

Paul quit gawping and instead gave him a confused look. "I hurt you. Why aren't you mad? Why did I—I can't do this if I'm going to turn into some wannabe killer!"

"Oh now, stop that," Justice said. "You're only killing the afterglow. This here"—he touched his wound—"is something every mate longs for. Well, every shifter mate, at least. It might be scary to our human mates."

Paul scowled at him. "You long to be bitten, to be bloodied and hurt?"

"When you put it like that, it sounds bad," Justice admitted. He winced when Paul merely gave him an arch look. "It's a mating bite, a claiming, as such. You made me yours, marked me for other males to see that I'm—" He just stopped himself from saying owned. It was true, but the word might rattle Paul. "Committed to you." He shrugged and winced again. He needed to remember to not do that until the bite healed a bit. Hopefully, though, Paul would mark him again, soon. "It's painful when it happens, I guess, but by the gods, talk about the orgasm to eradicate the memory of all prior orgasms. I almost passed out, it was so intense."

Paul went back to looking confused. "So that..." He gestured at the mark. "That's really a shifter thing? You're not just saying that so I don't feel bad?"

"Look." Justice tapped his temple. "You can see whether or not I'm telling the truth."

Paul's complexion had almost returned to normal, but at that he went white. "I can tell...in your mind?"

That might have been a mistake to point out, but it was already done, and Justice wouldn't lie to his mate anyway. "It's the mate-bond. Sometimes it's very strong, and other times couples barely register that it exists, I guess." *"But you can feel me, hear me even, can't you?"* Justice sent all the warmth and affection he could in the thought, wanting Paul to know it was okay—better than okay.

Paul landed with a thump on his ass. Justice saw the dark stain his cum had left on his jeans. He brought his attention back up to Paul's face. It was time to move them forward before Paul gave in to any doubts he had. "I'm not trying to freak you out. I can't just leap into your head. I wouldn't. I'll always—from this moment on—let you make the first move with that part of the bond, just as I have and will with the sexual part of it. But I'd really like you to come eat dinner with me. I'm starving."

Justice's relief when Paul stood and waited for him to rise was so great he could have swooned.

"I hope you can cook. I can't, and Marybeth said she was going to town for supper at the diner. Vivian went with her," Paul told him as they began walking to the cabin.

"I'm never gonna be a chef, but we won't starve." He wished he could put an arm around Paul, or just hold his hand, but he was afraid to push. He told himself to be happy with what he had, and he was. Things would move along as they should. He just had to have faith.

Chapter Eight

The next few days were hell, there was no other way for Paul to describe it. He had daily sessions with Vivian, even though she told him it might be better to set a twice-a-week schedule.

But Paul wanted to be better *right the fuck now.* He'd lost over two years of his life to the human traffickers. Even once he'd been freed, the acts of violence they'd perpetuated on him had controlled him. He was sick of it, sick of rolling in self-loathing and self-pity.

He talked to Vivian until his throat ached and he was actually ill. He talked when he wanted nothing more than to curl up in a ball and cry—and he did that, too. But he had too many horrible things to deal with to wipe it out easily.

Every day, he found himself needing to reach out to Justice more and more. At first he avoided their mental link. Despite his prior envy of his brother and Nischal's closeness, Paul was freaked out by the mental part.

It didn't help that he knew he'd already overshared with Justice. That first day when he'd come apart and had a panic attack while talking with Vivian, it had been him reaching out to Justice. What if he'd shared...everything, that had been zooming through his head?

Paul quickly got over being embarrassed by the possibility. He suspected he had done just that, and Justice hadn't been disgusted nor had he treated Paul like he was damaged goods.

"It's going to take time, Paul," Vivian told him again, for what was probably the tenth time. "We've only had five sessions. I really think daily is too much. It's bringing up issues faster than we can deal with them effectively. Rushing is only going to make things worse. Isn't this session kind of proving my point?"

Since he'd just had another horrible panic attack, Paul was inclined to agree. "But I want—" He stopped and wiped at his eyes. Then he took a drink of water from the bottle Vivian handed him. "You don't understand, and it sounds so fucking crazy, but...Justice is leaving tomorrow. I don't—" Yeah, it was going to sound as crazy out loud as it did in his own head. "I don't think I want to be here without him."

Vivian's eyes bugged before she quickly moved to sit beside him. "Paul, that's an extreme attitude, and I know mates hate being separated, but talking about killing yourself is taking it too far, don't you think?"

Paul scowled at her. "Get your head out of the graveyard, Vivian. I meant I want him to stay." Or he wanted to go with Justice, but he didn't know how to bring the possibility up, and he knew Justice wouldn't. Everything was up to Paul.

"Funny," Vivian said dryly. "I did leap to a wrong conclusion, sorry. Justice can't stay, you know that. He has his job, and it means a lot to him."

"More than me?" Paul asked, feeling like a petulant asshole as soon as he said it. "Never mind. I know he has to work, and that he loves his job. I wouldn't want to make him feel like he had to choose, I just wish he didn't have to go." He eyed Vivian. "Don't you live with him?"

Vivian eyed him right back. "Okay, session over. We are no longer in therapist-patient mode. Now I'm simply Jus' sister, and you're his mate."

Once Paul nodded she continued.

"Okay, yes, I do live with him, but only for another month or so, and I'm sorry, but I really don't think it'd work well with the three of us there and me being your therapist. That would be stretching the lines between us too thin, don't you think?"

As much as Paul wanted to tell her he didn't care, he did. He had to, because what he was and what he wanted to be were still too far apart. "Yeah, I get it." It just sucked. "Once you find your mate, you'll understand how hard something like this is. I want to be with him all the time, but I can't. Sometimes I need to be alone, and think, and after these sessions, I feel like shit. If I hadn't seen the mate-bond in action with Preston and Nischal, I'd think I was developing some kind of new psychosis, but I know it's just the pull between mates. Preston can hardly stand to be away from Nischal for even a few hours. He can do it, but God, does he bitch and whine about it."

Vivian laughed and set aside the pen and tablet she'd still been holding. "Yeah, some mates are like that, especially at first. But reality generally demands a separation—people have to work and eat and pay bills. I think Preston and Nischal are still in their new, lovey-dovey phase." She touched his hand. "I know it's going to be hard, but it will give you even more incentive to work at getting better, right? And Jus will come down on his days off, if he can get a flight. The man isn't broke, he saved most of his military pay, he told me so."

Then she tapped his hand. "As for the psychosis, that's a bit harsh. Do you know what psychosis is?"

"God damn it," Paul muttered as he rolled his eyes. "I thought I did, but apparently I was wrong."

"It's defined in the DSM-5 as a disorder in which a person loses touch with reality. I don't think that was quite what you meant."

Paul gave her a narrow-eyed look. "You're the kind of little sister who is always right and has to have the last word, aren't you?"

Vivian blinked at him, her expression one of innocence. "What other kind of little sister is there? We all have chips on our shoulders, don't you know?"

"Not really. I only have a twin brother." Paul looked at his fingernails. They could use a buffing. "At least that wasn't as bad as the last one, the anti-social bit."

"Yes, there's a big difference between being unsociable and being anti-social." Vivian stood up. "I'm pretty sure you're not the latter."

"I don't think I'm a sociopath, either, but it's nice to know you believe in me." He stood as well. "I'm going to go try to take a nap. I'm meeting up with Justice for an early dinner, then he's going to try to teach me to play some game, Bioshock Infinity, Infidel, something. It's a game, and there's an 'I-n' to part of the name."

"You two have fun. Remember," Vivian slipped right back into her therapist mode. "No guilt. What you two do is completely different than anything from your past."

"I know." And he did. It was different from anything he'd even done before being abducted and sold, different from those sweet young men he'd liked to mess around with. What happened between him and Justice was deep and...*and meaningful in a way those other relationships never were.* He truly felt like Justice was a part of him, the other half of his soul. Love wasn't in full bloom, but the seed was planted and Paul could imagine it growing into a vine that bound them happily together. "Thank you," he said to Vivian as she walked to the door. Paul followed and locked it behind her once she left.

If he could ever get over all his hang-ups and issues. He got so horny for Justice at times, but since that day he'd attacked him in the grass, Paul had held back. Despite hearing from Marybeth, Vivian, Preston and Nischal that the mating bite was normal, it still freaked Paul out a little that he'd so completely lost himself to his desires. He didn't even remember making a conscious decision to bite Justice—he'd just done it.

And God, it'd felt *so* good! The salty flavour of Justice's skin, the coppery tang of his blood—and that was disturbing, or it should have been. Paul couldn't quite regret it, and that worried him.

There was so much to learn. He was working past his fear of shifters. He wasn't afraid of Justice, Vivian, Nischal or Marybeth. Snow leopard shifters weren't the breed that had hurt him, and he didn't think he had a problem with them.

Wolf shifters, however... Everyone could tell him they weren't all evil, but Paul couldn't accept it. He didn't want to meet Oscar's mate, ever. Shit, he still worried about that third, unknown shifter who'd attacked Terence and Pat. What if he came after Paul?

There were others still out there, too. Paul decided he needed to be more proactive. Well, more would imply he'd been proactive in the first place, and he hadn't, but it was time to start. He'd call the FBI agent in charge of his case tomorrow, and see if she'd learnt anything new.

He was wrung out from the session and wanted a nap, then a shower. Actually, he wanted Justice, but he wouldn't seek him out. They had a date of sorts planned, and Paul didn't want to cut into whatever it was Justice was doing.

The temptation to prod through their mental link was strong, but Paul had to admit, he really needed the nap. He went to his room and collapsed on the bed. Within minutes, he was dozing, his mind in that not-quite-sleep phase. He wondered idly what Justice was doing.

Honestly, he hadn't meant to intrude, and he wasn't sure Justice was even aware of him poking around. Not when Justice was hovering at the edge of orgasm, his mind filled with images of Paul—his face, his hands, his soft skin. That last thought was definitely Justice's. Paul didn't pay attention to his skin except to glare at his freckles.

As if that thought reached through to Justice—and it might have, Paul had to admit—Justice groaned loudly. An image of Paul's freckled face, then his shoulder, stilled in the maddening swirl of pictures. Paul felt Justice's climax rising. He flopped onto his back and quickly shoved a hand down his jeans. His inhibitions vanished and he wanted Justice there, wanted Justice's hand on him. God, he wanted Justice *there!*

"Give me two minutes, honey, and I'll be knocking at the door."

Hearing Justice's voice in his head was comforting and sexy at the same time. More than getting off, Paul wanted to just see Justice, and maybe, maybe, have Justice hold him.

Paul took his hand out of his pants. He got up and though he probably should have went to the bathroom and washed off any vestiges of tears that had dried on his skin, he didn't. There was nothing he wanted to hide from Justice. Nothing he should hide. Justice had almost assuredly already seen his darkest moments that first day when they'd connected mentally. What could be worse than that?

Paul made his way to the door and stood there, one hand on the deadbolt, the other hand on the doorknob. He stared out of the peephole with one eye closed as he waited. Justice came into sight at a full run, wearing nothing more than a pair of cargo shorts. Sunlight reflected off his sweat-slicked tanned skin. His chest heaved as he sawed his arms back and forth, setting off ripples in those mighty biceps. Paul wished Justice was naked so he could see his thighs bunching, his cock bobbing. Still, he had a damned fine man to watch.

A flick of the wrists had the lock turned and the doorknob twisted. Paul stepped back as he opened the door. Justice leapt onto the porch, landing almost at the doorway.

Paul did what he'd ached to do—he opened his arms.

Justice moved so fast he was a sexy blur of man and comfort. Paul was holding him, wrapping his arms around those broad shoulders and resting his head on a rock-hard chest in an instant.

Justice murmured soothingly and lightly stroked Paul's back. Paul held his mate tighter, and to his mortification, a sob slipped free.

There were many things Justice could have done, like pick him up, coddle him, spew banal words that really meant nothing in the face of Paul's pain. He didn't. Instead he just held Paul, and hummed softly as he rested his chin on Paul's head. Those slow, gentle touches to his back never ceased as Paul tried to compose himself. He didn't want to keep falling apart. He wanted to be strong for Justice, and for himself.

When he finally thought he had all the day's ugly feelings out, Paul sighed and nuzzled against Justice's chest. "Thank you," he croaked, his throat aching from what he'd put it through then and earlier in the therapy session. It'd been a day of relieving some of his most horrific injuries, ones that still scarred his skin. Paul had been stressing over Justice seeing them and thinking him hideous, because the ones that had got infected, or had been reopened just for his torturers' enjoyment, looked nasty still.

Pink and puckered, jagged, thick, Paul hated every fucking scar they'd given him. Justice could probably feel them through his shirt, if he pressed a little harder.

But Justice kept his touch light. Paul didn't want him to. He wanted Justice to touch him so he'd ask Paul about the scars. Bring it up first, because Paul didn't know how.

Justice slowed his caresses down. He kissed the top of Paul's head, then he unerringly settled one hand on the worst scar. "I know where they are, Paul. I felt them when you came into my arms. They don't matter to me. They won't make you unattractive, but I can't guarantee I won't be very angry when I see them. Can't guarantee I won't want to kill the shifters who did it to you."

"I want to kill them," Paul ground out. He needed a drink, badly. "Kitchen?"

"Anywhere you want to go," Justice told him. He eased away and Paul reluctantly let go of him.

"I'm sorry I lost it like that. It's been a rollercoaster day for my emotions." Paul looked at Justice's hand. Could he hold it? *Well, why the fuck not? I've touched his dick, twice.* Paul slid his hand in Justice's and started towards the kitchen. Justice curled his hand around Paul's. "I was explaining the scars to Vivian, and how I'd gotten each one. How much I dreaded showing you them."

"There's no rush, and I told you, the scars won't change the way I see you."

Paul glanced at him and started to speak, but his voice cracked. He walked to the sink and had to let go of Justice then so he could grab a couple of glasses. Justice took the ice trays from the refrigerator and popped some cubes lose. He dropped them in the glasses, then Paul filled them with water. He handed one to Justice.

"Thanks." Justice brought the glass to his lips and drank deeply. Paul watched and probably drooled, he was so entranced. He swiped at his mouth and chin, relieved to find no saliva on either. He took a drink of his own water.

"You know I meant what I said, no pressure," Justice informed him, setting down his glass.

"I know, but you're going to leave and I…" Paul took another drink before setting his glass on the counter. "It's stupid, but I feel like if you leave, something bad will happen, either to you, or to me."

Justice tenderly stroked his arm. "That's our bond. It's hard on mates to part, especially like we are, with nine hundred miles soon to be between us. The thing is, a mate wants to do what's best for his other half. That means, right now, me going back to Phoenix, and you staying here."

"But—" Paul began, only to close his mouth. He knew Justice was right.

"On top of the therapy, which I hope is helping, the fact is, you're safer here. Levi and Lyndon will be back tomorrow, along with Oscar and Josiah. I know that might not be a good thing to you right now, but I've met Josiah before. I swear to you, he's a good man," Justice said earnestly. "He is. Not a cruel bone in his body, and maybe, if you give him a chance, you'll be able to see that it's wrong to blame the whole breed of shifter, just as it'd be wrong to blame a whole race of people if a few of them had hurt you."

"They scare me," Paul admitted quietly. "I hate it, hate being scared. It makes me feel weak, and I know that I am when compared to a shifter. I mean, look." It was easier to whip his shirt off over his head and present his back to Justice. "How can I forget this? I can't even stand to look at a damned Chihuahua!"

To his credit, Justice didn't gasp or growl or anything like that. He was as quiet as a statue. Paul dared to glance over his shoulder.

Justice traced the worst scar, the one where Terence had ripped through skin and tissue with sharp claws.

"He wasn't even in human form," Paul scraped out. The shame of that admission, of what had been done to him regardless of his begging and pleading, was threatening to take Paul to his knees.

Justice did make a sound then, like he'd been stabbed with a dull blade between his ribs. He moved and in one step he was plastered against Paul's back. "It wasn't your fault. You don't have to feel ashamed, Paul. They should. No decent person, whether human or shifter, takes advantage of their strength and uses it to harm others. That you're here, and whole, and in my arms, is proof of how much they underestimated you. Your strength is greater than theirs. It's greater than anyone I've known."

Paul was going to cry again if he wasn't careful. Justice's words were a balm to his wounded soul, at least temporarily. Whether or not they'd stick was hard to tell. Paul turned around in Justice's arms. He looked up at him.

"Kiss me?" Two words, but they meant so much. Paul was asking Justice to lead, to take control, at least for the moment.

Justice bent down and brushed his lips back and forth over Paul's. Paul closed his eyes as he settled his hands on Justice's shoulders. He parted his lips and moaned when Justice kissed him properly, the way he wanted, with tongue and divine pressure. At the same time, Justice began caressing his back again with those gentle touches that were unravelling all of Paul's worries and insecurities. At least the ones in regards to Justice wanting him still.

Justice's tongue licked into his mouth, teased and twined around Paul's. Paul rose up onto his toes, seeking more. More what, he wasn't sure, but he knew Justice wouldn't fail him.

Justice slid his mouth down Paul's chin and nibbled at where his jaw met his ear. Paul shivered at the delicious sensation, then Justice was moving again, lowering himself down as he licked and kissed a path to Paul's right tit. Paul opened his eyes and looked at his nipple.

There were scars there, too, where he'd had rings put in against his wishes. Having them torn out had fucked with his sensitivity there, but Justice's mouth still felt amazing when he began to suckle the scarred flesh.

Paul cupped his hands around Justice's head, not pulling, only holding on. Justice used one hand to gently pluck at the other nipple. Paul could barely feel it, and he growled in frustration.

"Harder?" Justice asked.

Paul bobbed his head. "I think so. I don't know. The scar tissue, the damage there, I can't feel as—oh God!"

Justice had pinched and nipped with enough force that it made Paul's knees weak as lust shot from his tits to his ass, then to his cock and balls. He curled his fingers against Justice's short hair and panted as his nipples were given plenty of attention. Paul's cock ached for a touch. It leaked pre-cum as Justice kept stimulating those taut nubs.

"Please," Paul rasped, afraid he was going to fall over.

His pants were opened with a quick move of Justice's hands. The second Justice's lips touched his cockhead, Paul gasped and hunched over Justice's head. The move drove his cock farther into Justice's mouth.

Justice hummed, his approval obvious in the sound and in the way he tapped Paul's hips.

Paul wasn't going to last, and his willpower was shot. No one had sucked him off raw in ages, and even so, the past blow jobs couldn't compare to the tight, wet seal around his cock now.

A deep thrust in, given slowly, had his crown breaching Justice's throat. Justice swallowed and Paul pulled back, loving the drag of those wet muscles around his shaft. He thrust back in, slow, deep, not stopping until his balls were pressed to Justice's chin.

That was the rhythm he kept for as long as he could, which wasn't long at all. His balls soon drew up and his body warmed, blushing with arousal and his impending orgasm.

Paul sped up just a little as he ran his hands up his chest and pinched at his tits. He had to do it pretty hard to feel it, but that was okay, it was damned good.

He tipped his head back and moaned as Justice tongued his slit. That was something he liked and hadn't experienced before. Justice did it again, then he came off Paul's dick. Paul started to protest, but his balls were licked and sucked and that felt fucking amazing.

Justice sucked on his sac then took Paul's cock in to the base. He growled or rumbled somehow, and Paul's world was well and truly rocked. He came so hard it was like a punch to the gut, knocking all the air from his lungs as he shot his load.

Justice suckled, moaning off and on until Paul finally pulled his dick from Justice's mouth. Justice fumbled with his shorts.

"Let me," Paul said. Justice stilled his hands. Paul pushed them aside and unfastened the first button. "I want to suck you."

"Gods," Justice groaned. "If you say that again, I'm coming to make a mess in my shorts."

Paul shoved the material down, pleased that Justice had gone commando. Justice's cock was thick and long, uncircumcised. Paul hadn't even noticed before, but he hadn't exactly been studying Justice's shaft last time he'd seen him naked.

"Beautiful," Paul said as he carefully eased the foreskin back. "Look at that beautiful prick."

Justice leant back, slapping his hands to the floor behind him. "Please, Paul. Touch me, do whatever you want, but let me come."

"I'm not stopping you," Paul murmured. He dipped his head down and sniffed, taking in the odour of Justice's need. Then he licked over the leaking slit.

"Fuck!" Justice's arms quivered.

Paul raised his head. "Lay back before you fall. I sure don't want that happening when your dick's in my mouth."

Justice cursed again and pinched his shaft. "I'm too close," he offered by way of explanation. He eased himself down and manoeuvred his legs until he was flat on the floor.

Paul eyed his dark balls, the skin wrinkled and plum-coloured. He leant down and licked over them and Justice shivered as he parted his legs.

Paul hefted his balls in one hand. He pulled them up and saw the tiny, tight swirl of Justice's asshole. Had anyone ever fucked Justice?

"Paul," Justice whined, moving his legs restlessly.

Paul licked up the length of Justice's cock. He took the head in and sucked until his jaws ached. With one hand, he stroked Justice's nuts. As he took in more of his length, he moved his hand lower until his fingertips brushed over that hidden spot nestled between Justice's cheeks.

The moan that got him was intriguing. Paul rubbed that hole with a little more pressure as he flicked his tongue along Justice's length. Justice didn't thrust— the man had more self-control than Paul ever would. Paul waited until he was able to take Justice into his throat before he pushed the tip of his finger into Justice's pucker.

Justice made a garbled sound and his cock swelled in Paul's mouth. Paul felt the thickest vein on the underside throb against his tongue and he raised his head, keeping only the crown in his mouth as he wiggled his finger in deeper.

Justice thrashed and his cum spurted in hot jets of salty, bitter liquid. Paul drank it down, almost sobbing with the relief of actually tasting his mate. His finger was gripped by those soft inner walls. Paul wished he'd had more time to explore Justice's ass. He'd have liked to have found his gland and driven him wild that way.

He eased his finger out then rubbed over Justice's ring until he knew every wrinkle of that snug hole. As much as he'd have liked to suck on Justice's cock all day, he finally let that thick length slide from his mouth. Justice's shaft wasn't even soft, but then again, neither was Paul's.

What he wanted wasn't another round of sex just then. He wanted to sleep, and he wanted to do so with Justice. "Come to bed with me?" he asked.

Justice took his hand. "Anything you want."

Chapter Nine

A week, that was all it'd taken for Paul to become the most important part of his life. Justice even considered taking a leave of absence or quitting his job just so he could stay with Paul. That wasn't rational, it was foolish, but the intrinsic need to be with his mate was very powerful.

Justice wasn't going to quit a job he'd always dreamt of having. Paul wouldn't want to live at Grandma Marybeth's forever. Vivian wouldn't either, though she would remain behind to work with Paul. Justice wished he could stay and help Paul through the healing process, but he'd be there as much as he could. Hopefully their mental link would still be possible over the miles separating them.

He was going to miss the freedom to run, too. Justice stretched his legs, taking bounding leaps through the dense foliage. It was another bright, sunny day but the trees sheltered him from most of the heat. The sun's rays slipped through and dappled the ground with bits of yellow and white. There was a slight breeze, just enough to keep everything interesting, bringing

Justice scents of rodents and larger animals along with the verdant plants growing in the area.

There was even the hint of water on the air. Justice chuffed at that. It'd be a good day to play in the stream. Paul was with Vivian, and Justice needed to keep his own mind in a state of easy flow. He didn't want to add to Paul's stress.

Paul hadn't wanted to go today. It had filled Justice with a warm fuzzy feeling to know that Paul wanted to spend the entire day with him, but his duty was to make sure Paul had what he needed. Paul needed the sessions with Viv and Justice wasn't going to be selfish.

At least he was outside, smelling the crisp forest air, hearing the birds sing in the distance. There were other sounds, too, the clicking and whirring of insects, the scurrying of tiny feet and panicked heartbeats. Justice didn't intend to kill anything during his outing. He'd eaten well beforehand, remembering his hesitancy over the buck.

So he had his full belly, and was feeling lazy even as he loped along. It'd been a long time since he'd had such a sense of contentedness. Runs were rare in Phoenix. Nonexistent, really. He had to take trips to neighbouring mountainous areas so he could shift and run. That took time he didn't always have. His work schedule varied, but he rarely had two days off in a row. Maybe once he had more time in, that would change.

It was going to make it difficult to visit Paul, but he'd do what he had to, for them. It occurred to him that Paul might be willing to fly to Phoenix and see him. That was something they needed to discuss. They'd been spending most of their time together talking about everything but their parting. Justice was going to step up and see what compromises they could reach.

He heard the splash before he saw the bear. Since the animal was upwind of him, Justice hadn't smelt the beast first. He supposed the bear wasn't concerned with his approach. Justice slowed down. He had no interest in fighting a bear. He watched while the bear splashed in the stream. What would Paul think of this? There was a beauty in nature, even the scary parts of it like the huge bear. Justice hoped Paul would be able to see that, if not now, someday soon. *It would be amazing to bring Paul with me on hikes, to share this with him.*

Of course Justice wouldn't want Paul anywhere in the vicinity of a bear, but the rest of it, the sunlight and sounds, the aromas and feel of earth beneath one's feet, that he wanted to share.

But Paul had yet to see him in shifted form. Justice feared his mate might never be able to accept that side of him. He mewled and the bear swung its big head his way. Justice expected a roar, but what he got was an inquisitive sound as the critter eyed him.

In case he was looking like a possible dinner, Justice thought it was in his best interest to vacate the area. He'd play in the stream another day, perhaps.

Running would put the most space between him and the possibly hungry bear. Justice put his powerful hind legs to work and was far away before the bear's roar stopped ringing in his ears.

The hair along his spine stood up as he stilled. Someone, or something, was watching him. A predator was a predator for a reason. His senses were heightened and danger was riding in on the breeze.

Justice kept moving, slowing his pace gradually. He sniffed at the air every few seconds, and when he finally caught a whiff of what was tracking him, fury and fear collided inside him.

Wolf. Not just a wolf, but a shifter. God damn it! Had the sick fucks who'd been part of the human trafficking ring found Paul? The FBI agent, De la Garza, had told Paul they hadn't been able to find any more of the people involved, but Paul had admitted to Justice that he hadn't told them much, if anything, about the shifters. Justice understood. Who was likely to believe shifters existed, unless they were one, or mated to one?

The scars had been explained away as from wolves, kept as pets. Like Paul had been. It made Justice sick, but dwelling on the past wasn't going to help them now.

The chances of there being a wolf shifter on the property or near it, and that shifter having nothing to do with Paul, was nil.

Justice walled off the part of his mind focused on the other shifter. He didn't want Paul to pick up on it and have a panic attack or be scared. Up ahead, the shrubbery thickened. If Justice could slip into it, he'd possibly be able to circle around and get behind the wolf. It was an obvious ploy, at least to him, but he couldn't come up with a better one at the moment.

Paws struck the ground behind him. His stalker was no longer trying to hide his presence. Justice knew he wasn't going to be able to make it to the bushes and he spun around, head low, growl tearing from his throat. It was times like these he wished to hell and back that he could roar like a lion, but snow leopards weren't given that gift. Marybeth had claimed it had to do with avalanche prevention in their homeland. *An avalanche would be great right about now.*

What had to be the largest wolf he'd ever seen came charging at him. Big, grey, with one gold eye and one silver, the beast was frightening. His teeth were huge, sharp, and saliva was dripping from them.

Justice's heart thudded, adrenaline shooting into his veins as he prepared to be attacked. He snapped at the air, warning the wolf, not that he thought it'd work.

The wolf came at him—and yipped before bouncing to a stop. The damned thing lowered his upper half and wagged his thick tail.

What the fuck kind of crazy is this? A dozen possible theories ran through Justice's head, but they all had the same conclusion—this was a setup.

He snarled and swatted a paw through the air. Dying wasn't an option, not on his part, anyways. He snapped again and lowered himself, preparing to leap on the wolf.

But the damned thing whined and wagged his tail again before flopping over and baring his belly. Even then, his tail kept swishing against the ground, kicking up dirt and leaves. His tongue lolled out of his mouth, the tip landing on the dirt. Those mismatched eyes held a serious note, but not a cruel one.

It didn't make sense. Justice growled and sniffed. He smelt wet dog, or wet wolf, which wasn't a pleasant odour as far as he was concerned. There was nothing in his senses telling him this was a trick, though his leopard wasn't thrilled to be so close to any kind of canine.

The wolf yipped at him then whined and wiggled. Justice narrowed his eyes at the thing. Sunlight glinted off something on the wolf's neck and it made Justice squint as he found the source of the shiny. A strip of thin black leather was around the wolf's neck, and dangling from it was a small glass jar filled with stuff.

Justice didn't know what kind of stuff, but it looked like dried green plants and pebbles, maybe even a tiny piece of feather. Or hair.

There was something about it that was mesmerising. Justice jerked his gaze away from the necklace. That was some freaky kind of mojo or something in it. He wanted no part of it, even if he was just being ridiculous and the necklace was nothing.

Before he could do anything else, the wolf began to shift. That gave him pause. There was no way a man could outfight or outrun a snow leopard. To turn into his human form now would mean the wolf shifter was completely vulnerable to him.

Why would he do that? What's his game?

Justice didn't have time to look around and check for more wolves because the man had shifted in no time at all. He didn't seem to have hurt when it happened, either. And he was fucking huge in human form, too, with more bulk than Justice could ever hope to attain. Loose black curls hung unevenly around the man's face. He still had those mismatched eyes when he looked at Justice and grinned.

"Did I scare you?" he asked in a deep, rough voice. "That's good," he answered before Justice could. "I wouldn't want you to be cocky, not if you're going to be Paul's mate."

"What the fuck?" Justice tried to say, but that didn't work out so well in his leopard form. He sounded like a cat trying to hack up a hairball. Was this a trick to get him to shift? Did the weird stranger think that Justice wouldn't be able to kill him if they were both humans? A smaller stature didn't mean a weaker man, Justice had learnt that ages ago.

"You are Paul's mate. That's good, makes you protective of him and he'll need that in case they come for him still."

Fuck it, I'm shifting. He'd be vulnerable for a few seconds, but that was a risk he had to take.

The pain of shifting didn't even register this time. Justice tried to keep his eyes on the wolf shifter, but there was a few seconds where his vision hazed and his ears filled with an annoying buzzing. Then he was on his hands and knees, doing his best not to show any signs of exertion.

"That looks like it hurt," the man rumbled, sounding amused. "Must suck to be one of your kind."

"Who are you?" Justice snapped, wishing he'd just killed the bastard in the first place.

The bigger man smirked and sat back on his heels, looking as if he knew Justice's thoughts. "Most people call me Cliff." He shrugged. "That's one of the nicer names. But I'm not here to be your best friend, Justice Chalmers. I'm here to make sure none of the shifters involved in the trafficking ring get to Paul. I have some — excuse me, can't word it any other way — justice to mete out to those shifters. We can't have that kind of shit going on in our world."

Justice leant back and glared at Cliff. "How do you know who I am? And what are you, some self-appointed shifter avenger?"

Cliff kept smirking at him. "Well, I could tell you that there's a super-secret shifter society that handles wayward dumb fucks who put all of our kind at risk."

Justice thought Cliff was just screwing with him, but he wasn't a hundred per cent sure until Cliff let loose a braying belly laugh.

"Gotcha." Cliff chuckled again then wiped at his left eye, the silver one. "Do my eyes freak you out? Usually I wear brown contacts—"

"I don't care about your goddamned eyes! What game are you playing?" Justice snapped the question out as he curled his hands into fists.

"No game, other than seeing how huffy I can get you," Cliff told him. "I killed two of the bastards who were after Paul. Got there just in time, too. You should thank me for that and stop being such a dick to me."

"You—" Justice looked the man over. The necklace caught his eye and he quickly turned his gaze up to Cliff's face. "You're telling me you were the guy that kept Terence and Pat from taking Paul?"

"Taking him, hurting him, killing him. Yup." Cliff stretched out his arms. Muscles rippled all over his body. "Killed Pat quick, then took a little longer with Terence. Fucker was too stupid to die easy." He shrugged. "Oh well. By my count, there's still about seven shifters waiting to be held accountable for what they've done. It wasn't just Paul, you know. There were several humans bought and sold and killed."

"How do you know any of this?" Justice asked, sceptical as all get-out.

Cliff winked at him. "You've heard the saying, if I told you, I'd—"

"I'm a Marine, of course I've heard it, and if you think I'd let you kill me, you're crazier than you seem."

"That'd have to be pretty far out there, then," Cliff replied. "I'm still not giving away my secrets. I will say I've made it my life's goal to protect our people, no matter what breed they are. The shifters involved in the trafficking exposed what they are to humans who are now free. A few of them are, anyway. A lot of them were killed as soon as the FBI started making busts."

"Where are the other humans? The ones who got away?" Justice asked.

Cliff sucked on his teeth then shook his head. "Nope, sorry, not telling. I know you're a cop and all that, but the less people who know, the better for them, right? You can't break under torture and give info you don't have. And before you say you wouldn't break in the first place, yes, you would. You'd do anything to protect your mate, even if you hated yourself for it."

Justice looked away. He knew Cliff was right.

"It's our nature to protect our mate above all others. I've seen it happen time and time again, and that's as it should be, but this time it could get innocent people killed. Really, you don't need to know the information anyway."

"No, I don't," Justice admitted. "I hope they're safe."

"They are," Cliff assured him. "I'm an ornery, wily son of a bitch when I need to be, which is most of the time. Have to be, or I'd have been killed a long time ago."

Justice looked at him again. "So you're a vigilante."

Cliff shook his head, then he nodded. "Whatever rocks your boat. If it makes you feel better to apply a term to me that I'm sure you look down on, go for it. But you and I both know that shifters, though they live on the same planet as humans, still live in their own world, with their own societal rules. It has always been that way, and do you think, Justice, that I'm the first of our kind to do what I do?" Cliff rolled his lips in, as if he were working to keep back more words. Maybe he was.

"Why are you here? And why should I believe you?" Justice settled for asking.

"I'm here because Paul is here. I know he would hate me on principle, so I can't very well go up to him and warn him. If I tried, your grandma would gut me." Cliff flashed a wicked grin. "Nothing in any world like a strong woman. Anyway, he's the only one left loose, so to speak. The other former slaves are safe, happy—some have even found mates who are shifters. Even wolves. It's weird, but whatever, Fate knows what she's doing. Paul needs to be watched, because the bad guys are going to come for him."

"I'm supposed to go back to work the day after tomorrow. I was going to leave in the morning…" Justice mumbled.

"Might want to rethink that," Cliff said, sounding entirely too amused. "Of course, I guess it's hard to let go of a long-held goal once you've attained it. I mean, the job you always wanted, or your mate's safety—"

"Could you be any bigger of an asshole?" Justice snapped. "And how do you know anything about what my goals are?"

Cliff tapped the small jar on the leather necklace. "Because I'm special."

"I'll say." That was just creepy. Justice hadn't missed the way that glass sparkled when Cliff touched it. "Are you a shaman?"

Cliff snorted. "Hell no. I'm not a 'pure' enough soul for that. I kill people who need it, Justice. I know that rubs your lawman side the wrong way, but it is what it is, and it always has been what it's been."

"Now you're speaking in fucking circles."

"It's a habit," Cliff said. "Look, the truth is, you have a hard choice to make, but you and I both know what you'll decide to do. You have to, he's your mate.

Maybe, once things settle down, you can get on with the local police or sheriff's department, whatever these bumpkin towns have. Your priority now is your mate."

"What are you going to do?" Justice asked him. The whole conversation seemed surreal, yet Justice was strangely relieved to know he wasn't going to be leaving Paul behind after all. He could take Paul with him, but there would be more people to help keep him safe here.

"I'm going to do what I've been doing for some time." Cliff stood. The man really was massive, but it surprised Justice to find the man was only a couple of inches taller than him.

"How is Paul doing?" Cliff asked. He wrapped his hand around the jar.

"It's going to take a lot of work, but he's up to it. He's a strong man," Justice said, proud of his mate.

"Good. Well, I don't imagine he'd be comfortable with someone like me hanging around, even out here, so I'll be moving on. If I can, I'll make sure none of the shifters looking for him finds him. Unfortunately, there's only one of me. I can't be everywhere at once." Cliff grinned, and before Justice could make a scathing comeback, Cliff shifted and took off, yipping like the goofiest wolf in existence.

Justice knew better. He'd felt the power the man wielded, and that whole glowing shit was weird.

He had other things to dwell on, however. Paul was going to argue with him about leaving his job, but… Maybe they'd get to have make-up sex.

That in itself would be worth giving up his job.

Chapter Ten

He'd known it was probably going to be a fruitless effort to have a session with Vivian when all he was able to think about was Justice leaving. The idea that something bad would happen to one or both of them if he did leave was preying on Paul's mind.

Vivian had mentioned coping skills and possible OCD. Paul didn't have obsessive-compulsive disorder. He just wanted his mate.

Paul closed his eyes and let that word roll around in his head. He murmured it, at first soundlessly, then softly. Justice had come to mean so much to him in such a short time. It shouldn't have been possible, but it had happened.

It was too bad humans didn't have such bonds. How many heartaches would be spared, how many marriages and divorces prevented? If you knew there was possibly a soulmate out there, waiting to find you or to be found, rushing into a marriage wouldn't happen.

Humans as a whole weren't so lucky. Every day, Paul would treasure the gift he'd been given. His fear of shifters was still there, but not of snow leopard shifters. Justice and his family's kindness was greater than Paul's fear.

Wolf shifters, however, were still nightmarish abominations as far as he was concerned. Maybe that would change once Oscar and Josiah were back. Paul wouldn't be able to avoid Josiah forever.

Maybe just until I can join Justice in Phoenix. I could stay in my cabin all the time. With Justice gone, I won't be sitting outside, the grass beneath me and the sunlight warming my skin while I wait for him to return. Damn, I'll miss this.

There was an odd sort of tension coming from Justice when Paul reached for him through their link. Something was bothering Justice, and it wasn't only their impending separation. Paul could feel the worry coming off his mate. He sat up and shaded his eyes with one hand as he looked at the brushes from where Justice always emerged after a run.

Paul heard Justice first. The heavy thud of paws on the ground, then silence before the unnerving sound of him shifting. Jesus, it sounded like it hurt.

Justice emerged minutes later, sweaty and sexy and so beautiful in his masculinity that it made Paul's heart race. "How was your run?"

Justice walked over, his cock already hardening, bobbing with every step. Paul dragged his gaze up, following Justice's treasure trail to his sculpted abs, then up farther to his taut nipples. By the time he reached Justice's face, his own erection was begging for attention.

"We need to talk."

"God damn it," Paul grumbled. "Four words sure to kill a hard-on."

Justice snorted and held a hand out to help him up. "Sorry. Didn't have an adverse reaction on my dick, though."

"Mine either," Paul admitted, "But it's making me nervous as hell. Nothing fun ever follows those words." He slipped one hand in Justice's. "What's wrong?"

"Let's go inside," Justice murmured as he surveyed the area.

That in itself unnerved Paul. "Okay."

Once they were in the cabin—Justice's this time— Paul leaned against the locked door and pulled Justice to him for a kiss. He didn't remember enjoying kissing so much when he'd been younger. It'd been part of the steps to getting laid, so he'd done it and it'd been okay, but nothing like this.

He felt Justice's kisses all the way down to his toes as he curled them against the wooden floor. Justice moaned and rested his hands on Paul's hips. Paul did a little shimmy that moved him closer. They could talk after they fooled around, couldn't they?

But Justice ended the kiss with sweet little pecks to Paul's lips. Paul protested by grabbing Justice's nape and trying to get more pressure.

"I'm not going back," Justice murmured against his lips.

That slapped Paul right out of horny-land. He jerked his head back and thumped the door. "Ow. What?" He was trying not to let out a celebratory whoop over that news. "No, no, you have to go. You love your job."

"It's a job I can do somewhere else, too, if they won't grant me an emergency leave of absence."

Paul looked into Justice's eyes, searching for regret or anger, and saw none. "You can't just give it up, Justice. Do you think they'll allow you to take off?"

Justice hesitated, then shook his head. "Honestly, I don't, but what I realised is, I can't leave you. I was dreading it, trying to convince myself that it was a crazy thing to do. My leopard, he was chewing me a new one. Turns out I should listen to my critter sometimes. You're my priority, and leaving won't make either of us happy."

"You staying won't make me happy, either," Paul argued, even though he wanted nothing more than for Justice to stay. "It won't make you happy, either."

"I'll be less unhappy than if I went to Phoenix," Justice countered with.

Paul frowned at him. "Don't confuse me. You have to go back." He held onto Justice a little tighter before he realised what he was doing, then he let go. "Seriously, you'll regret it if you don't."

Justice rubbed his nose alongside of Paul's, rumbling softly. *"No, I won't. I'll be distracted if I go, and that's never something a cop should be. I'll check the agencies in this area and the surrounding ones. Maybe I can find something here."*

Paul pushed him back. "You're distracting me, and you know it. Why would you look for a job out here? Are we staying here for a while? Did I get asked if that's what I wanted?" God, some of his forgotten flounce came back as he spoke. Paul cocked one hip and flapped a hand. The gesture and pose felt so familiar, it made him snap his mouth shut in surprise.

Justice stared at him fondly, his mouth curving into a sweet smile. "Preston told me you used to be more…uh."

Paul hated to see that smile vanish, so he didn't take offence. "I believe he used to say I had the swish and he had the sense. So not true. I've seen him prance for Nischal. He works those hips and Nischal follows him, leaving behind a trail of drool." The hard tone eased from his voice, and something in Paul's chest loosened. "I also have more sense. That's just not debatable."

"You're fucking perfect," Justice said. "Gods, Paul. It doesn't matter if you swish or swagger, you're perfect."

That was just too sweet. Paul was going to melt into a puddle of pure happiness. He would have, except for the whole job thing.

"We don't have to stay in this area, either. I shouldn't have presumed. We can go back to Denver—"

"No," Paul said sharply, his happy mood sinking. "Not Denver. They found me there."

"About that," Justice began before clearing his throat. "We really do have to talk."

The serious expression Justice wore scared the shit out of Paul, but he wasn't a coward. "Okay. Should we maybe have a seat first?"

"That's a good idea." They walked to the couch and sat beside each other. "I met someone in the forest today. I want you to listen to me before you react or make up your mind about anything."

"That doesn't sound good at all, and who would you meet in the woods?" Paul frowned. "I know it wasn't someone bad, because you aren't freaked out and trying to pack me off. Although, you have suddenly decided to stay—"

"The shifter who saved you in Denver," Justice cut in. "That's who, and he is a wolf shifter, but he's not—"

Paul tried, he really did, but hearing that there was a vicious wolf shifter nearby sent him into a panic attack. His chest went painfully tight as his lungs seemed incapable of getting enough air. Sucking in short, quick breaths didn't help, but Paul couldn't seem to stop it. His fingers and toes tingled as the lack of oxygen began to affect his appendages.

Paul's heart raced erratically. His head spun as his thoughts scattered. The loss of control was unbearable. He wouldn't give in, not again. Stronger, he was stronger than the panic attack.

It wouldn't defeat him. Paul tried the techniques he'd been working on with Vivian, and being able to somewhat get a handle on it helped his mental state greatly. He wasn't as weak as he had been.

"Paul, honey, please," Justice murmured. His presence in Paul's mind was comforting. "He isn't one of the bad guys. In fact, he kills the bad shifters who put our kind at risk."

So it wasn't about Paul himself, but about the risk to shifters. Paul bobbed his head.

"You're what it's about for me, not all the other shifters in the world," Justice continued. "I don't care what's happening on that level, not right now. I only want you safe, and happy."

"What did he look like?" Paul got the question out, needing to know in case Justice was wrong and the shifter was one of the ones who'd hurt Paul.

"Taller than me, black curly hair. He had a gold eye and a silver one, it was weird as hell." Justice grunted. "He was a smartass, too. Said his name was Cliff."

Paul stopped wringing his hands—*when did I even start doing that?* "Cliff? The shifter who approached Preston and Nischal at a rest area in New Mexico, his name was Cliff. I don't remember them mentioning that he had weird eyes."

"He said he wears contacts," Justice explained. "And what is this about him talking to Preston and Nischal at a rest area?"

"He talked to Sabin first, I think, if I remember the story right." Paul scratched at his head. "Something about he had followed them and wanted to make sure everyone was safe and happy and he was…" Paul stopped and searched his memory. "Oh my God! He gave Preston—no, Sabin—a paper with the address to the house I'd been kept in! He knew things, but he…but he…" Paul had to stop and put his head between his knees and just breathe.

"He's on our side. I believe that. He said some things, I don't know." Justice caressed his back. "Made me think there was more to who he was and what he did than I'll ever know."

"Did he really kill Terence and Pat?"

"Yeah, he says he did. Maybe that should bother me, but it doesn't. I'm glad they're dead, and anyway, human justice and shifter justice aren't the same thing. Not at all. I wouldn't condone going out and killing like he did if he were a human, but there is no regulating government or police force in the shifter society."

"Except for this Cliff," Paul added as he sat up, no longer fearing he'd pass out. "I don't want to meet him."

"He said he was moving on. He just wanted to make sure you were okay, and—" Justice sighed and rubbed at his face before looking at Paul. "He says there're more of the assholes who hurt you, and they're looking for you. There's no way in hell I'm leaving your side. Not for a run, not for anything, Paul. I can't. Please don't think I'll let them get you."

Paul was trying not to have a complete freak-out. Damn it all, he was tired of falling apart! It'd been almost a year since he'd been freed, yet he wasn't free, not really. Fear held him in a tight grip.

"I want a weapon, something that will take down a shifter," Paul said. "I'm sorry, but I do. I need to be able to defend myself."

"I won't let it come to that, but yes, I think that's a good idea. Do you have any experience with guns? Tasers?" Justice asked.

Paul huffed out a little laugh. "I know guns can kill and Tasers scare me as much as a gun does. That's the depth of my knowledge."

"That's a good place to start. We'll go from there." Justice stood and stretched, grunting as bones popped. "Let me go call the Chief, see what he says. I can't tell him what's going on, so whatever happens, happens."

Paul stood too and pressed his head to Justice's chest. "I don't want you to lose your job. Let's just go back to Phoenix. This is both of us, so I should get a vote in what happens."

Justice cupped his chin and waited until Paul looked up at him. "If I had to leave you at the apartment all day, or night, depending on my shift, I'd be worried the whole time I was gone. Even if you had a gun, or a Taser, you could still be hurt by someone. I'd never be able to stand it if that happened, and I could have prevented it by staying here for a while, where our family can help us remain safe. Just like you wouldn't be able to handle it if I were hurt on the job because my head wasn't in the right place."

"Guilt, your weapon of choice," Paul grumbled. "And damn it, you wield it well. I would totally fall apart if you were hurt because of me and my stupid pride."

"So we can stay here for a while?" Justice asked softly. "It might be weeks, months, longer even, before the wolf shifters are dealt with."

Paul bit his bottom lip. The slight pain helped push back the threat of panic so that by the time he quit biting himself, his voice was calm. "Whatever it takes, right? So we're both safe."

* * * *

"It went better than I thought it would," Justice said as he turned in his chair to look at Paul. "Chief Warren said he'd try to keep my spot open. Not sure he bought Grandma needing me here to help her out, but at least he didn't flat-out call me a liar." Lying didn't sit well with him, but he couldn't very well admit the truth.

"Maybe it will be over soon." Paul stood and strode over to him. "Come on, that pizza you put in the oven should be done any minute now."

"The timer—" Justice began right before the annoying sound of it hit the air. "Done."

"Ugh, what a racket," Paul grumbled. He ran to the stove and swatted at the timer button. "Next time it can burn."

"Viv would love that. She still at Grandma's?"

Paul nodded. "Yup. Toss me an oven mitt?"

Justice spotted one on the table. He grabbed it and tossed it to Paul. "This kitchen could use a paint job. It'd be pretty done in a pale gold."

Paul looked at him like he'd come unhinged. "Why would we want to paint it? The white's fine. This whole cabin is nicer than any apartment I've ever lived in. I love the wood floors, and walls, and ceilings—it's like Ultra-Manly-Ville in here."

"I like it too, but the kitchen seems too dark. Kitchens should be sunny and bright, plus I'll be doing most of the cooking." It seemed like a logical point to him.

"Well, since it is going to be your domain…" Paul took the pizza out of the oven and set it on the stove top. "Pale gold sounds good to me."

A key in the lock warned them of Vivian's arrival. Justice hurried to the front door just to make sure it was his sister on the other side of it. Once he saw Viv through the peephole, he relaxed and opened the door for her. "Hey, sis, did you have fun at Grandma's?"

"She said you better get your ass down there to see her before you leave," Vivian said as she stepped inside. "Is that pizza? Aw, man, I just ate liver and onions."

"That's disgusting," Paul called out from the kitchen. "Seriously, I might have to rethink having you as my therapist if you're going to eat shit like that."

Viv cocked her head and gave Justice a surprised look. "He sounds a lot more…cheery than I expected, considering you're leaving in the morning."

There was no point in delaying, although he did only want to go through the whole story one more time. "About that. Do you think you can get everyone over here? There's some important things I need to tell y'all and I don't want to have to do it more than once. Twice, since me and Paul have already talked."

Viv studied him for a moment then sighed. "Maybe we should just all go back to Grandma's?"

"No, see if she will come over here instead, along with Nischal and Preston. Are Levi and Lyndon back?"

"Not until next week," Viv said. "Oscar and Josiah will be here tomorrow. They can't handle being away any longer. You know Oscar's a real homebody."

Something occurred to Justice then. "Hey, isn't he supposed to be something like the family guardian? Didn't I hear something about that?"

"You did, why?" she asked.

Justice grimaced. "Because I think we're going to need him."

"Tell me what's going on."

"Pizza's served," Paul said as he came out of the kitchen. "Vivian, let Justice eat. He's not gotten the chance to since his run, and no matter how much he eats before he shifts, he's always starving afterwards." Paul pointed at him. "You should eat a warthog or something. Couldn't be as vile as liver and onions. Oh! Let me put some napkins on the table." Paul went back into the kitchen.

"We don't have warthogs in Colorado." Justice thought, quickly. "Or in the U.S. I think." Then it dawned on him—Paul had just made an easy reference to him being in shifted form, letting his leopard have his way and hunt. That was a step forward, a big one, he thought, but just to be sure, he sent a questioning look to Viv.

She grinned and gave him a thumbs up. "Warthogs are indigenous to Africa!" she hollered at Paul. "Eat, brother mine, and I'll get everyone over here. You owe me for being patient."

"I'll save you a slice of pizza, and promise not to tease you about your breath." Justice darted away, laughing as he escaped his sister's punch.

Despite the seriousness of the coming discussion, he was happy. He wouldn't have to leave Paul, and he hadn't been fired, yet. That was better than he'd hoped for.

Chapter Eleven

"I like your family—the ones I've met—and I love my brother, but I am so glad they're all gone."

Justice nodded. Even Viv had left, saying she'd bunk with Marybeth and let 'the boys' have the cabin. Justice had refrained from snarking that he was older than her and neither he nor Paul were boys. She'd been trying to yank his chain. "Me too. Gods, you haven't even met all my other siblings."

Paul gave him a startled look then burst out giggling. The sound wasn't one Justice had heard from Paul before, but it suited Paul. Paul ended the giggles on a snort that had him looking horrified. Then it was Justice's turn to laugh.

"It's not funny," Paul huffed. "Snorting is so undignified when you're laughing."

"It's cute," Justice countered. "What set you off?"

Paul's cheeks darkened. "Well, see, when I first found out your name was Justice, I kind of made a bitchy comment about that and, er, possible names for any brothers and sisters you might have. But I was mad, and scared," Paul stressed. "I tend to revert to bitchiness at such times."

"Really?" Justice dragged out, raising one eyebrow at his mate. "I had *not* noticed that at all." It was fun being able to tease Paul, who rolled his eyes dramatically and turned his little nose up in the air. "I like that part of you too, so it works out well. I think I'll probably even be making you mad just to see you get all huffy."

"You're doing a good job of it now," Paul informed him. "I hope you have siblings with names like Mark, Frank, Betty. Well, not Betty. That was the name of my boss at the museum I worked at a few years ago. She was a real annoying person, all hyper and happy all the time. It was unnatural. Whatever drugs she was on, she wouldn't share, either."

"Those kind of people always freak me out," Justice admitted. "Like their brain is always stuck in Happy gear, and they have the energy of a toddler."

"Exactly," Paul agreed. "How many sibs do you have?"

"Six," Justice informed him. "Mom and Dad would have had more, but things didn't work out that way. I'm the oldest, and yeah, Justice. The only one of the kids with a unique name because I was born the year Dad got on at the Maricopa County Sheriff's Department. Also, I'm the only one Mom let Dad name. She said he got one chance, and while she loves me, Justice isn't a name she'd ever have saddled a kid with. Hence, in birth order, Joel, Bennet, Aaron, Clive, Vivian and Henry. She had us pretty much one right after the other."

"That's a lot. Geez, I can't imagine. It was always just Preston and me, especially once we came out. Our parents are pretty religious. They didn't handle it well." Paul shrugged. "They said they'd always love us, *but*. Any time there's a 'but', it means 'not really'. I haven't even seen them in years. Supposedly they were on their way from Hawaii when I was found, but they never showed up. I haven't even gotten a phone call from them, but—heh, yeah, I did get an email saying they hoped I was doing well. I didn't even reply."

"Maybe you should," Justice said after considering it. "I mean, be the better person and all of that, sure, but also, show them that your life is going well."

"It is," Paul said with something akin to wonder. "It really is, even with the issues I have and possibly being hunted, I'm still, well, I'm happy, mostly."

"Mostly is good, I'll take it." Justice rose from the chair he was in. Paul's furrowed brow stopped him from mentioning his desire to get clean. "What's wrong?"

"Nothing's wrong. I just realised that's a lot of boys." Paul held up one hand and started ticking off points. "And there's only Nischal and Sabin from their mom. Levi and all his siblings, there's a bunch of boys and only the one girl. Is that the norm for snow leopard shifters?"

"As far as we know, yes. There's actually a family in Mongolia, snow leopards and scientists. They've taught us a lot about our heritage and what we are. Females are the rarer offspring, maybe nature's way of keeping our population under control since the shifter ability is passed from mother to child." Justice added, "It's different with other breeds of shifters, but as far as I know, it's only one gender that can pass along the trait, either male or female. Ours is female."

"Huh. Interesting." Paul seemed a bit distracted. Justice knew how to get him focused.

"Now, I need a shower."

Paul's concentration centred on him immediately.

"Sounds like a plan, especially if I can wash your back." Paul gave him a flirtatious look.

"You can wash any of me you want to," Justice informed him, laying on the innuendo. He wanted — well, he just wanted.

"Any of you?" Paul asked. Justice nodded. Paul bit his lip, then let it go as he exhaled. He looked nervous as he stood there. Justice waited, not wanting to spook him out of asking his question. Finally Paul started twisting his wrist. He glared down at his hands. "Damn it, I hate that." Paul planted his hands on his hips, and a cocky expression had his lips tipped up on one side. "Can I play with your ass? Do you do that?"

Justice's dick sprang up hard and happy. "You've touched me there before."

"Yes," Paul dragged out. "Barely. You were so tight, I thought maybe you didn't do that."

Justice wasn't going to lie. "Not with anyone else, Paul. Ever. I never wanted to, but when you touched me like that, I just about came apart at the seams."

"You did come," Paul said as he leered. "I do remember that very well." He held up one hand. "Fingers are okay?"

"Yeah," Justice rasped after the second try.

Paul stuck out his tongue and wiggled it.

"Oh gods," Justice whimpered. "Definitely, that's definitely okay."

Paul chuckled and licked his lips. "What about..." He ran a hand down his own body to cup his dick. "Or is this out of the question?"

"Anything. Anything, Paul." Gods, he was going to beg for it like a slut. Already he was clenching his asshole with anticipation. "Fuck me."

Paul's eyes went wide and his mouth dropped open.

Justice started backpedalling. "You don't have to. We've never even discussed doing anything like that. I shouldn't have just blurted that out, but like I said, I never let anyone—"

"Move," Paul got out as he all but wrapped himself around Justice. "You can't just ask me to fuck you then stand there. *Move.*"

They stumbled and groped their way to the bathroom. Somehow they got their clothes off along the way. The shower was large, one thing Grandma Marybeth had insisted on when she'd had the cabins built.

Paul plastered himself to Justice's front, hooking a leg around one thigh and wrapping his arms around Justice's neck. "I'm going to turn you inside out, baby," Paul said, and Justice shivered. "Might even have to do this again." He nipped the bite mark that had almost healed up. "I think I'm getting over being freaked out by it, 'cause I need, so bad." He sucked on the spot.

"Fuck!" Justice got his arms under Paul's butt and hefted him up. While doing so, he turned and got his back against the wall. He was hoping it'd keep him from collapsing. His eyes rolled back as Paul scraped his teeth over that spot repeatedly. Justice cupped the back of Paul's head. "Please, honey, gods, do it!"

Paul rumbled wordlessly. He shoved a hand down between them and gripped Justice's dick. Then he bit, and he used his hand to squeeze Justice's cockhead. Justice's orgasm slammed into him with no warning. He loosed a strangled yell as his cock pumped out his pleasure.

"I feel like a vampire," Paul said a short while later in between licking the bite mark. "I like it."

"Me too." Justice gave himself a mental shake. "The biting, I mean. I like it." But he couldn't ever see doing it in return, not when Paul had been bitten and clawed at—no, his leopard longed to mark his mate, but it wouldn't happen.

Paul raised his head and unwound his legs. He got his feet on the ground. His dick stood thick and hard, pointing almost straight up. Paul pressed it against his stomach. He looked at Justice. "I want to fuck you, but—" He shook his head.

"But what?" Justice asked. "I can get hard again, no problem. I want you to fuck me, so again, no problem, and I thought we agreed those 'buts' were bad things."

Paul sighed. "It *is* a bad thing, Justice. I want to fuck you, and you've never let anyone do that before, so you've always considered yourself a top. I can't promise you that I'll ever be able to let you do it to me. I wish I could. I hate that this isn't equal between us."

Justice ran his fingers along Paul's jaws. He loved the golden stubble there. "The thing is, I don't care if I never fuck you. We don't even have to do this—you don't have to fuck me. Plenty of gay men don't engage in anal sex, and we don't have to. There's lots of other ways we can pleasure each other. I don't feel like this is unfair, or like I'm losing out if we don't have anal sex, or if you fuck me and I never fuck you. It's the passion between us that I want to share."

"You'll tell me if that ever changes?" Paul asked. Justice nodded. "Okay. I really do want to fuck you. I didn't do that often, and never bareback. I can't imagine how good you'll feel on my dick." Paul touched the bite mark. "And this? I know you feel the same urge. When you're about to come, things just flow right into my mind. I even heard your leopard being all snarly."

"I won't bite you." Justice wouldn't.

Paul canted his head. "What if, someday, I want you to?" he asked. "Or maybe I'll want you to try it when we're not having sex. Make it an act independent of sex, see if I really do want it or if I'm getting my urges tangled up with yours."

"I won't bite you, unless you're sure," Justice amended. "I can control it."

"You're a better man than me." Paul stretched up onto his toes. Justice bent down and they met for a tender kiss. "Still up?" Paul fondled Justice's cock. "Yeah, you are. Let's have some fun."

* * * *

Jesus, he was going to be lucky if he lasted long enough to fuck Justice. Paul grabbed the soap and a washcloth as Justice started the water. He wanted to touch every inch of Justice's body before they got lost in each other.

"Water temp good for you?"

"It's fine," Paul said as he got the cloth wet. "Put your hands against the wall and let me have my way with you."

Justice laughed and turned around. "Which side?"

Paul eyed the very nice, thick cock pointing at him. "Uh. This is good."

Justice leant back and braced himself against the tiles. "I'm all yours."

Paul licked his lips and started. He washed Justice's face, careful not to get soap in his eyes, then worked his way down. He didn't tease—much—but they both enjoyed what he was doing, especially when he cleaned Justice's balls and cock. "Turn around," he murmured, giving those balls a lingering touch.

Justice basically rolled over, giving Paul his backside. When he pushed his well-muscled ass out, Paul whimpered and stroked over the firm mounds. Justice had a very nice, big bottom covered with just the right amount of hair.

"Feels good," Justice said.

Paul agreed, felt divine. He left off groping and washed Justice down. "Rinse, then let me do your hair."

Justice followed the directions without comment. Paul shampooed his hair then had him rinse that out, too.

He took Justice's hands and placed them back on the tile. "Put your left foot up on the rim."

Justice did, panting slightly with excitement. Paul reached between his legs and stroked his dick. "So hard."

"So fuckin' horny," Justice retorted. "How can you stand it? You haven't come once yet."

"Because I want to come in your ass, and that's worth waiting for." Paul ran his hand down Justice's length. He palmed his heavy balls and rolled them.

Justice moaned and arched his back, tipping his ass up. Paul traced his crack with his other hand, and kept playing with Justice's nuts. Until it wasn't enough, not for him, or Justice.

He left off touching Justice's sac and brought both hands to Justice's butt. "Love the way this feels," he said as he began to knead the globes. "God, so fucking much."

"So do I, but I need more," Justice told him in a stripped voice.

Paul pried his cheeks apart, exposing his tiny pucker. Water ran down Justice's crack. "Turn it off." He figured Justice knew what he meant.

The water was shut off and Paul leant forward. He licked his way down Justice's spine, holding his ass open. When he reached the top of Justice's crack, he knelt and let himself follow that furrow right on down to the sweet pucker he longed to taste.

Paul licked over it and Justice gasped. That was a good sound. He licked again, dragging the flat of his tongue harder against that tender flesh. That got him a louder gasp.

Paul licked and nibbled that outer ring, listening to the sounds Justice made, letting them guide him as to what to do more of, and what to skip from then on. There wasn't much of the latter. Justice was clearly enjoying the hell out of being rimmed.

Even when he gently scraped his teeth over that sensitive skin. Paul did it again, then he stiffened his tongue and began thrusting against the tight ring.

"Yes!" Justice bellowed. Paul would have grinned, but at that moment the resistance ceased and he stabbed his tongue into Justice's hole. Justice went wild, jabbering and writhing for him. Paul pulled back and used his thumbs to press at Justice's opening. He leant back farther and spotted the conditioner. Neither of them had thought about lube.

Paul pressed the tip of his thumb into Justice's ass. He stood and used his other hand to grab the conditioner. Between his teeth and his free hand, he got the stuff open. He tipped the bottle upside down and poured it right down Justice's crease. Seeing that thick white stuff slide down his crack just about did Paul in.

He used it to slick his fingers, running them through the viscous liquid. When he had Justice's hole covered, it was the most erotic sight he'd ever seen. Paul moaned and removed his thumb from the tight opening. He immediately pushed a slippery finger inside. The hot grip was maddeningly perfect, as was the needy sound Justice made. Paul sank his finger in as deep as he could.

"Good?" he asked.

Justice's answer was to push back on his digit. Paul grinned and began finger-fucking him, slow at first before picking up speed. "More?"

He didn't wait for an answer, not when he could feel Justice's need throbbing inside him. The second finger went in with little resistance, though he was careful not to push too fast or let Justice spear himself on the digits.

And Justice was trying, moaning and cursing, writhing like sex incarnate. Paul curled his fingers and angled them just so. He brushed over Justice's gland.

Justice yelped and bucked harder, seeking more. Paul gave it to him, slipping a third finger in and touching his prostate repeatedly.

He could smell Justice's pre-cum, the salty, tangy odour of his need. Paul nipped on his butt cheeks, leaving behind pink spots that faded quickly. He reached around and fisted Justice's dick at the base, holding it tight. Justice growled, undulating with an urgency that was beautiful to behold.

"Ready for me?" Paul twisted his wrist, giving Justice's rim a good stretch. He kept the pressure light, letting Justice's body and feelings guide him. With the link flowing open between them now, he was able to know and feel what Justice did. It was making it damned hard to keep from just fucking the man through the tiles.

In answer, Justice pulled himself off Paul's fingers by turning sideways. He went down on his knees, bending over the side of the stall and putting his hands on the floor.

When he looked back over his shoulder at Paul, the hunger in his expression made him seem a primal being, lost in his body's needs.

Paul slicked his dick with the conditioner still on his hand. Justice's hole was plenty lubed and it gaped slightly, waiting to be filled. Paul knelt and lined his cock up. He gripped Justice by the hips and pushed into the tightest, hottest grip he'd ever sank into.

Justice moaned and mewled, spreading his legs wider to offer up more of his ass. Paul thrust in to the balls and wrapped his arms around Justice's body. Desperation prodded him to thrust, but he waited until he was sure Justice was ready. Paul kept the movements short and hard, not wanting to release Justice so he could withdraw farther. He hammered into Justice like that, staking his claim and revelling in the feel of being inside his mate.

Justice made a garbled sound. Paul managed to get a hand back on Justice's shaft just as his balls drew tight. He teethed whatever skin he could reach while forming a fuck tunnel with his hand. Justice humped it, keening almost non-stop.

Then his cock swelled and those sweet, gripping inner walls contracted around Paul's shaft. Justice moaned and shook, cum spurting from his slit, some of it getting on Paul's hand. It was too much. Paul grunted and ground against Justice's ass as he climaxed.

It seemed to go on forever. Paul was lost in that moment of perfect ecstasy, carried to the heavens and left with the bright evening stars.

Eventually he came back to Earth, back to his mate, who was panting beneath him. Paul collapsed on Justice's back. He needed a few seconds to catch his breath and get the strength to stand up. Plus, he loved the way his softening dick was being massaged by Justice's body.

Eventually, his cock slipped free and Paul shivered. He got to his feet and held out a hand to help Justice up.

Justice looked startled. He hitched up a leg and reached down and back. "It's leaking out. That feels — it kind of tickles."

Paul started the shower. He didn't mind at all if he got to wash Justice off again.

Chapter Twelve

Running through the forest and around the mountains and hills was out of the question. Justice wouldn't leave Paul alone. When Paul had therapy with Vivian, Justice either sat out on the porch or did something around the cabin. Family members had been returning home, but so far, they'd stayed out of sight.

Justice knew there was more family coming in. It was what they did—circle the wagons and protect their own. There was even some bigwig shaman coming from Josiah's brother's pack. Remus. Justice had heard of the man, and he was kind of intimidated. He also wasn't sure why the shaman was coming, but Grandma Marybeth said he was and Justice wasn't going to question her. He'd likely end up with an ear twisted off if he did.

Since it was a nice day outside, and Justice was feeling a touch of cabin fever, he was sitting on the porch steps when he saw movement out of the corner of his eye. He tensed but relaxed once he spotted Oscar making his way over.

"Hey." Justice waved at him. Oscar had always been hard for him to read, mainly because they didn't know each other well. Justice had been in the Marines for almost half of Oscar's life. He'd missed a few family reunions then when the military said time off was a no-go, but even when he'd made it to them, Oscar hadn't been very approachable.

Oscar stopped in front of him. "Can I sit?"

"Sure." Justice scooted over since he was sitting in the middle of the steps. Oscar would have fit beside him. Unlike most of the people in the family, Oscar wasn't as tall or bulky. He also had lighter hair and generally didn't resemble the shifter side of the family. He'd lost the tips of two fingers in a bear trap back when he was a kid, but Justice never really paid that any attention. He'd seen men blown to pieces while serving his country. Two fingertips were nothing to gawk at.

"What's up?" he asked.

Oscar tipped his head up, staring at the cloudless sky. "Maybe I'm just being friendly."

Justice snorted and nudged him with an elbow. "Right, Oscar. I can count on one hand the number of times you've ever come up and said hi to me."

"Same goes," Oscar pointed out. "So we're both assholes."

"Guess so," Justice agreed. "Doesn't really make it okay. I'm reminded every day how grateful I am for having such an awesome family."

Oscar did look at him then. The smirk the man wore bespoke of mischief to come. "I do make up a good percentage of that awesomeness."

"I think you're confusing yourself with me." Justice could joke, too. "I mean, I did ten years in the Marines, and that right there equals boss-awesome."

"It equals you getting old," Oscar snarked. "Whereas I am still in the bloom of my youth."

"You're a blooming something," Justice agreed. "I'm leaning towards idiot, because if I'm old? What would that make Grandma? Shit, she'd beat your ass."

Oscar narrowed his eyes. "You'd better not narc."

Justice held out his hands. "Wouldn't dream of it, bud." He put his forearms on his thighs and let his hands dangle. "Seriously, what's up? I'm glad we're talking and all, and hey, glad to know you can dish it out and take it, but I get the feeling that's not why you're here."

"It's not, and you're smarter than you look." Oscar sighed then groaned. "Shit, I need to learn when to turn the smart-ass off."

"It is difficult. Got my ass in a bind a time or two in boot camp before I caught a clue. Couldn't fight with all my strength, either, because I was scared as hell they'd figure out I was a shifter somehow." That was how Justice had learnt a large part of his self-control.

"I'd rather not have some pissy Marine kick my ass, so I reckon I'll just have to try harder." Oscar glanced away, then back at him. "I know Paul is scared of shifters, or at least wolf shifters, but here's the thing. I can't keep Josiah hidden away. This is his home, too, and he shouldn't have to stay in our house all the time. Although, we are having a hell of a lot of mind-blowing sex." He shook his head. "No, even so, he's afraid he's going to step out onto the porch and scare your mate half to death."

Justice tried not to be affronted. Oscar was as protective over his mate as Justice was over Paul. "He doesn't have to stay inside. I just want to know when he's out on the property so I can keep Paul away from him." Oscar looked at him. "Wow, that does sound kinda crazy," Justice conceded. "This mate business is tricky, isn't it? You want to do what's best for them, but I sure as hell don't always know what that is."

"Fear is a powerful owner," Oscar said. "It controls us if we let it. I know, believe me, I know Paul has been hurt by wolf shifters. Somehow, the word has gotten around to Josiah's pack, even. I swear there's no bigger gossips in the world than shifters."

"Paul would hate that, having everyone know. He's so ashamed." Justice tried to tell him not to be, but it was something Paul had to work through in his own time.

Oscar went back to staring at the sky. "Understandable. If it makes any difference, I sincerely doubt anyone's going to come up to him, ever, and share that fact with him."

"I'd hope not." Justice leaned against the railing, turning as he did so in order to watch Oscar. "So tell me, what do you think our options are? Because if you've never seen a panic attack—and felt one, because believe me, our mental link brings those bitches slamming right into me—then you can't understand why I want to prevent Paul from having them if I can. Wolf shifters, damn, Oscar. He has scars—" Justice stopped. He wouldn't go into any further detail about those. "He has every reason to be scared. Logic, that just doesn't play a part in it. His brain knows that blaming an entire breed for the actions of a few is wrong. His body, however, has the memories of why he should fear them etched into his skin."

Oscar went from staring at the sky to studying the ground. "I get that, I do, but fear that strong, it's a powerful thing. It could cause him to be hurt. Just think for a minute, just listen and let me speak."

How Oscar had known he was about to interrupt was a mystery, but Justice sealed his lips together and waited.

"If something happened to you, say you were sitting out here and someone shot you right between the eyes, killed you on the spot, and Josiah was the only one nearby to help? How would Paul react?"

"I can't imagine, because he'd know I was dead, and he'd be going out of his mind from that. I don't think he'd care what happened to himself at that point. I wouldn't if our positions were reversed." Then Justice corrected himself. "That's not true. I'd find who did it and kill them. Then I'd just go off and die."

"You're missing my point," Oscar growled. "Jeez, dude. If he needed help and Josiah tried to be there for him, Paul might freak out, hurt himself or Jo. He needs to try at least to accept his new family."

And Josiah was now a part of Paul's family. Justice hadn't even thought of it like that. "Maybe it'll make a difference, seeing it like that."

"Like what?"

Justice poked Oscar in the arm. "Like Josiah is family now. Paul mentioned that his parents basically ditched him and Preston when they came out. I think he only sees Preston, and maybe, *maybe* Nischal as family. That needs to change. He needs to know he has more family than he can shake a stick at now."

"Pretty sure he could shake a stick at any number of people," Oscar groused. "I have never for the life of me understood that saying."

"Yeah, well, don't disparage it. It's been around for ages."

"Doesn't mean it needs to keep being around." Oscar tipped his chin towards his own cabin. "So I was thinking, maybe we could have y'all over for lunch or dinner. I can tie Jo up if it'll make Paul feel safer. We'd both enjoy that, don't know about you and Paul."

"That is way too much info, perv. And before you tell me bondage doesn't make you a perv, let me say I agree. Telling your cousin about those kind of details, however..." He trailed off and laughed when Oscar flipped him the bird. "I'll talk to Paul. He's with Viv right now, but they should be finishing up soon. Hey. Aren't you the family protector or something like that?"

"Something like that," Oscar agreed. "Why?"

Justice arched his back. His ass was pleasantly sore from Paul fucking him earlier that morning. For a guy who'd never thought to bottom, Justice was quickly becoming addicted to it. He pulled his mind out of the gutter. "I guess I'm wondering why you're not out hunting down the wolf shifters who hurt Paul."

Oscar stood up and looked down at him. "It's my understanding someone's already doing that. I was told by Remus not to interfere in that. When Remus speaks, you'd best listen. The man is not to be trifled with. So here I am, protecting my family this way. We'll be starting patrols in the forest and all over the property tomorrow. I just haven't been able to get everyone organised yet, but damn it, I'll do so by this evening."

Oscar held out his hand. Justice shook it. "You let me know about lunch or dinner. Text, come over, e-mail, yell. Whatever."

"Will do." Justice watched his cousin jog off. Oscar wasn't as standoffish as he'd thought. Justice certainly bore more of the blame for them not being close, since he was the elder of them.

He was learning more about himself and his family every day. More about Paul, too. Paul was complicated, amazing, sometimes snarky, but at the core, he had a good heart. He'd lost himself when he'd been held as a slave, but he was discovering himself a piece or two at a time. Justice really liked the man emerging.

His cell phone buzzed in his pocket. Justice took the phone out and answered it, his pulse speeding up when he saw the Chief's number on the screen.

"Yes sir," he started with. Chief Warren didn't let him get any further than that.

"Chalmers, I'm going to have to let you go. I can't give you any more time. HR will have my head, the union will be on my ass and between the two, there won't be shit left of me to bury."

Justice was stunned. "But it was just a few days ago—"

"I know. Then Tommy Tompkins asked for time off, and I had to give it to him, didn't I? But Lewis Vidal wanted to know where you were and why you got so much time off when last year I wouldn't let him have more than his earned vacation time."

"Vidal's a dick." Justice had never liked the homophobic asshole.

"That may be so, but he had a point. I'm sorry. Maybe when things are straightened out with your granny, you can reapply. I can give you a glowing referral, too."

"Thanks, I'd appreciate that. If you could fax it to me, please." Justice wasn't taking any chances. He'd just got screwed. On the one hand, he understood why the Chief just pulled a reversal, but on the other, he wished his boss—*former boss*—had grown a pair sometime in his fifty or so years of life.

Then again, the position of Chief was more politics than anything else at some points.

Justice made sure Warren knew where to send the fax to. He didn't much care for anything the man had to say after that.

Now he was going to have to deal with finding another job. At least for the time being, he could concentrate on taking care of his mate. He had enough money saved that they could live frugally without either of them working again, but being idle wasn't something he could do for long. And yes, he imagined he and Paul could have a hell of a lot of sex, but they'd have to do other things in life as well.

Besides, Justice had been raised with a good work ethic. It wasn't all about the money. Being a productive part of society was good for a person, it helped build their self-esteem and show them the value of a job done right. Wasn't the news full of stories about rich kids who ended up doing stupid shit, and never paying as steep a price for it as poorer folks did?

Justice turned towards the porch when he heard the murmur of voices and the soft thudding of footsteps. The door was opened and Viv came out, smiling at him.

"Hey there, big brother. Coming to Grandma's for dinner tonight?"

Remembering Oscar's vow to get everyone organised by this evening, and his invitation to come over and share a meal, Justice wasn't sure what their plans were. "I'll let you and Grandma know in a bit. Oscar wants to get some sort of patrols going, like they did back when Levi and Lyndon were being stalked by Lyndon's father and brother."

"Somehow, I'd forgotten about that," Viv said. "Talk about a psycho dad. Just so you know, Grandma is going to end up coming down here and lecturing y'all if you both don't visit her soon. See ya!"

Viv blew him a kiss as she bounded down the steps. Justice watched her leave. Down the way, Oscar and Josiah joined her, no doubt because there was safety in greater numbers.

Assured his sister was in good hands, Justice walked up the steps and across the porch. Paul met him by the door, opening his arms for a hug. There were the usual signs of strain around Paul's eyes and mouth that were there after his therapy sessions.

"Anything you want to talk about?" Justice asked, not wanting to pry but willing to listen.

"Just more of the same. I didn't think talking about everything would help, but it has. Vivian is going to be a successful therapist. She's really knowledgeable and understanding." He raised his head up and smirked. "Almost like a totally different person outside of her job."

Justice snickered. His baby sister was something special. "Do you want to go for a walk?"

Paul tensed and averted his gaze. "Maybe later. I— Oh, what the hell. I'm not afraid of running into any of your family, per se, but the idea of doing so then having a panic attack? That scares the shit out of me."

"They're your family too, now," Justice informed him, getting to one of the points he needed to. "We're mates, Paul. That's even more binding than human marriages. My family is your family, all of them, and vice versa. I'm not just saying that, either. Look at how they're pulling together to ensure your safety, and mine, yes. Because they're our family."

"Well, now I feel like a jerk for being scared to meet them," Paul mumbled. "I—if I didn't know which one was the wolf shifter, I probably wouldn't freak out, but I'm afraid that's exactly what's going to happen."

"Maybe it will, maybe it won't. Oscar came by a little while ago. He seems to think that if we met with him and Josiah privately for a meal, it might help you to see that Josiah isn't anyone to fear."

"I don't think I could eat. They could come over?" Paul didn't look entirely sure of his idea, but he ploughed on. "Come over and we could sit on the porch swing, and try that."

"Oscar did say he'd tie Josiah up if it'd make you feel better." Justice recalled his cousin's lusty expression. "Pretty sure Oscar and Josiah would enjoy it."

That got a laugh out of Paul. Justice loved hearing that sound. Now he was going to have to bring it to a halt, because he wouldn't keep secrets from his mate.

Justice led Paul over to their porch swing and sat down. Paul joined him easily. "Chief Warren called and told me he was letting me go. Someone he'd refused extra time off to last year bitched about me being gone, so now I'm permanently gone."

"Oh, Justice, I'm so sorry," Paul said, cuddling to his side. "I'm just fucking everything up for you. Wait. Wait, that's very self-centred and selfish and all the bad self-stuff. I'm sorry for that, too. This isn't about me. Is there anything that can be done? Do you want to fight it?"

"No, I don't think so." Justice leaned his head back and stared up at the porch ceiling. He pushed with his feet and got the swing to moving. "I'd be treated like shit if I took on the department and won. I'd also never trust the chief again. Think I'd rather try a different department, maybe even the same one Dad worked at. If," he added, "you want to move to Phoenix. If not, I'll get on with some law enforcement agency somewhere."

"Phoenix is somewhere I've always wanted to visit. I think it'd be as good of a place as any to live. I love the desert. Well, the pictures I've seen of it. I'm not really attached to any one place, Justice, and you shouldn't have to give up the city you love."

Justice did love Phoenix. His mom, dad and siblings were all there. He knew where all the best places to go were, and he was comfortable there. "Thank you. I'd like to stay there."

He sighed, knowing there was one more point he needed to bring up. Justice rolled his neck, easing out a knotty feeling spot. "Are you afraid of me when I shift? Afraid to see me, I mean? Because those patrols Oscar wants started, those will be in shifted form. There's going to be leopards and a cougar, and maybe even Josiah roaming the grounds, though I am betting Josiah stays out of sight. And there's this wolf-shifter shaman coming, too, a guy named Remus. Supposed to be a really powerful man."

"A shaman?" Paul twisted around and looked at him. "He...does he—is he like the Native American shamans?"

"No idea, honey, I've never met him. Now that I think about it, I have heard Grandma Marybeth mention him before. Remus. How could I forget that name?"

"It's not a name I've ever heard before."

Justice hadn't either. "Well, at least I won't be the only one here with a different kinda name."

Paul placed his hand on Justice's knee and gave it a little squeeze. "I like your name. And about your shifted form, I honestly don't know. I guess I'd just have to see you like that." He took a deep breath, held it, then exhaled. "Maybe you should do that really soon, just to see how I react."

"How soon is really soon?" Justice asked.

"Now, maybe?" Paul got up and took a step back, closer to the door. "I'm not scared, seriously, but on the chance that I might lose my marbles, you should probably go out on the grass and do it. I'll start with standing inside at the window and go from there."

"Okay." Justice let Paul get inside, then he rose, set his phone on the swing, and walked away until he was closer to the forest line than not. He stripped off his clothes, glad he hadn't bothered with shoes. Paul stood at the window, watching him.

Justice knelt. He started shifting as soon as his hands hit the grass. The pain started in his spine and quickly spread out along his nerve endings. It was worse in the bones, that ache was deep and true.

Once he'd shifted, he dropped onto his belly and tried his best to look more like a housecat than the skilled predator he was. He flicked his tail and mewled, his gaze tangling with Paul's.

Paul hadn't run, but he was moving away from the window. That wasn't good, not at all. Then Paul disappeared. Disappointed, his leopard yowled, pained at his mate's rejection.

But the front door was opened, and Paul appeared in the doorway. He hadn't fled after all. In fact, he didn't look panicked. Wary, maybe, but not panicked.

They stared at each other until Paul took a step outside. Justice rolled over onto his back, writhing a bit to show his mate he wasn't a threat. He watched Paul upside down. Paul took a few more steps until he was standing on the edge of the porch.

"Come a little closer," Paul said quietly. There was only the faintest of tremors in his voice.

Justice rolled over again, and began what he hoped was a cute crawl towards his mate. Trying to wag his tail like a dog wasn't working for him, so he quit trying as he inched closer.

Paul's tentative smile was heart-warming. Justice wanted to see that every day, several times a day. He came closer, and still Paul didn't back away.

Paul came down the steps after a minute or two. He waited, hand out, watching Justice.

There was no way his leopard was missing out on an opportunity for an ear-scratching. Justice moved a little quicker, almost giddy to feel his mate's hands on him.

Then he was right there, waiting to take the last few steps. Paul licked his lips and closed the distance between him and Justice.

The instant Paul's hand was on his fur, Justice became a purring fool. His eyelids drooped and he raised his head up eagerly.

"Someone's a sweet, um, kitty," Paul said as he scratched that perfect spot right behind Justice's ear.

Oh damn, but it felt so much better when Paul scratched that itchy place. Justice couldn't quite reach it, and he'd almost torn his ear off a time or two trying.

"Yeah, who's a good kitty kitty?"

Justice stopped purring and opened his eyes. That was a little too patronising for his taste.

Paul raised his eyebrows. "What are you looking huffy about? Want me to stop scratching your ears?"

Justice mewled and closed his eyes. He wasn't an idiot.

"I think I can handle this," Paul told him.

Which was good, because Justice could handle being loved on in both of his forms.

Chapter Thirteen

The nightmare streaked through Paul's entire being. It wasn't just his head it messed with. He woke up, his own scream ringing in his ears. He gradually became aware of Justice's presence, of his arms around Paul, holding him.

"Sorry," he mumbled, as he always did.

"You have nothing to apologise for." Justice also gave his usual reply in that deep, sleep-rough voice.

"I'm sorry I woke you up." Except he was also glad to have Justice touching him, holding him. "Mostly."

Justice gave a deep rumble that Paul thought of as an internal laugh. It eased the remaining tension from Paul's body, and he snuggled in closer to his mate.

They sat cuddled together in the bed until both fell back asleep. Morning came and they almost missed it. Paul pried open his eyes and had to blink for almost a full minute until his vision was clear enough that he could read the time on the alarm clock. It was after eleven.

He didn't have therapy today. After agreeing to meet with Oscar and Josiah, Paul had had a short session with Vivian the night before. Today, there'd be tea on the front porch in the early afternoon, and time with Vivian if he needed it later.

Vivian was on the patrolling schedule now, but only for a couple of hours every other day. Justice wasn't worked in, but that was okay since Justice was with him.

There was definitely a nervous fluttering in Paul's stomach about the upcoming meeting with Oscar and Josiah. Intellectually, he understood that he couldn't blame a whole breed for what was done to him. It wasn't his intellect that was freaking out on him. Or threatening to.

He'd get through it. Justice had lost his job yesterday. Paul wasn't going to cost him his family, too.

God, he could use a distraction. He could just nudge Justice over on his side and slip right into that tight, hot ass. There was probably still lube from last night. Paul loved fucking Justice again after having come in him. It seemed so dirty and erotic, but it wasn't dirty. It didn't demean either of them.

Fucking Justice without a care for his pleasure, that would be demeaning. Paul wouldn't do that, not even to escape his own fears. It startled him to realise he was putting Justice's happiness and care before his own. For months, Paul had been lost in himself. Of course he hadn't seen it that way, but his selfishness had been truly appalling.

Yes, he'd been through some very horrible shit. Maybe his reactions were normal, if that word could be applied to the situation. Even so, it was time for him to really move past it. *No more trying*, he told himself, *it's time to actually do it.*

He wrinkled his nose. *That almost sounded Yoda-ish.*

Beside him, Justice stretched and yawned. Paul really did appreciate the show, all those muscles rippling, Justice's long limbs reaching out as he undulated.

Justice's dick was erect, pushing up at the sheet. Paul helped it get free, giving the material a tug.

"Mmm, s'a good start," Justice said in a scratchy voice.

Paul thought so, too. His own erection was going to have to chill, because he wanted to focus on pleasing Justice.

He started by rolling on top of that big, tanned body and licking the closest strip of skin. There was nothing like the taste of his man. Paul lapped at Justice's neck, giving it a good drag of teeth here and there. Justice was panting in minutes, clutching at the sheets and digging his heels into the mattress.

Paul nipped the bruised wound where he'd bitten deeper the night before. God, he loved the way Justice came apart for him.

He ran his hands up Justice's sides, then around to his pecs. Taut nipples tempted him and so he moved down and nibbled on one while pinching at the other.

Justice flowed like water beneath him, rippling and moving so smoothly in his need. Paul sucked up a deep purple mark above his right nipple, then marked the left as well. Justice's cock was leaking pre-cum between them—he was rubbing that thick length alongside Paul's shaft.

It took all of Paul's control to stop himself from grabbing Justice and rutting away to completion. Instead he worked Justice's nipples into dark, heated peaks as Justice writhed.

When those nipples were bordering on raw, Paul moved down to lick a path to Justice's cock. Along the way, he left a trail of purple love bites over ribs and chiselled abs. He delved his tongue into Justice's belly button and Justice clenched almost every muscle in his body as he made a strangled sound.

Paul grinned and laved that hole again before settling himself in a more comfortable position to suck Justice's dick. As close as Justice was, as hot as his desire and need was running, Paul wasn't going to tease any longer. Justice was going to come, soon, and Paul wanted that jizz in his mouth.

He pushed at Justice's legs then cupped his balls at the same time he sucked in Justice's crown. Justice jolted as if he'd been jabbed with a cattle prod. He had always kept still and let Paul control the depth and speed of the blow job. Paul revelled in having stripped Justice of that last bit of control. Justice's pleasure poured into him as that thick length sank farther into his mouth.

Paul moaned and despite his best intentions, he just had to fist his own dick. While he tongued the veiny shaft, sucked until his jaws ached, he also stroked his own cock and shared the pleasure of it with Justice.

Their lust synchronised, their ecstasy meeting and melding into one overpowering sensation. It covered them both as Justice shouted, driving his cock in, breaching Paul's throat. Paul swallowed and only had a second to appreciate the feel of his throat muscles holding in that heated length before he pulled back, his own shout muffled as he came.

Justice's spunk hit his tongue at that same moment, and Paul had never felt so complete as he did then, not even before he'd been abducted. Justice was so deeply entrenched a part of him, Paul couldn't imagine living without him. Couldn't imagine not having the affection and want between them, the laughter, tears and lust.

There was no way he would ever waste time even trying to imagine his life without Justice. He wasn't wasting any more time on what might have beens and what-ifs.

* * * *

So far, so good. Justice kept his arm around Paul's shoulders as Oscar and Josiah approached.

Oscar was walking in front of his mate, which made their height discrepancy more apparent to him. Then again, he was probably worrying over something stupid. Josiah would have looked taller than Oscar no matter where he stood, if he were by his mate. That was because Josiah was quite a bit taller than Oscar.

Paul stiffened slightly as Oscar continued approaching them. Josiah hung back, tucking his hands in his back pockets and staring down. It was an open, non-threatening position, and he pointed that out to Paul silently, using their mental link.

Oscar came up the porch steps. Justice wanted to stand, but he was going to let Paul decide what to do. Paul huffed and jabbed him in the rib, either accidentally or on purpose, Justice really couldn't tell. They stood, and Justice smiled at his cousin.

"I see you come bearing gifts," he said, gesturing to the jug of iced tea Oscar held. "Grandma's?"

"Yeah." Oscar set down the container and offered a hand to Paul. "I'm Oscar, and I tend to be blunt, so just tell me when I can let my mate inch closer."

"Ass," Justice said, tempted to bap Oscar on the back of the head.

Oscar glared at him. "What? Oh. Please. I always forget the please."

"I was thinking more along the lines that you sounded snarky and could use a paddling," Justice informed him. "But since you did say please."

Paul laughed, the sound not quite true, but he was trying. "It's, uh, I guess it's nice to meet you. I'm not really sure about that yet."

Oscar gave Paul an approving look. "A man who isn't afraid to be blunt in return. I think I like you already."

Paul let go of his hand. "Well, I don't have your shifter senses, so I need a little more time to make up my mind about you." Paul delivered it with a smile that made it clear he was teasing. "I, uh, I guess he can come over here. Josiah, I mean."

"Didn't think you meant our invisible friend," Oscar grumbled.

Justice popped him on the back of the head. "Ass."

Oscar glared at him. "If I didn't deserve that, I'd so totally beat your ass."

"No doubt." Justice was bigger, more muscled, but Oscar's wiry strength would seriously cut into Justice's chances of winning if they ever did spar again.

Oscar held out his hand towards Josiah, who began to walk their way. He moved slowly, checking on Paul's reaction every other step.

"I'm fine." But Paul trembled a little as Josiah stopped beside Oscar. Paul's breathing was faster, but he wasn't in the throes of a panic attack. Not yet, at least. Paul studied Josiah, who at first kept his gaze down, but eventually, Josiah looked Paul right in the eyes.

Paul fidgeted, rubbing his wrist with his other hand as he tended to do when he was nervous. Then Paul stood up a little straighter. "Hey," he said, pressing against Justice but keeping his voice steady. "I'm Paul, but you know that."

"Josiah." Josiah offered to shake hands. Paul hesitated but covered it well, sliding his palm against Josiah's. "Nice to meet you."

"Same." Paul went back to twisting at his wrist. "You don't look like any of the ones I…I knew before."

Oscar beamed, the big smile so uncommon for him that Justice gawked while Oscar preened. "He is a stud, isn't he? Never seen a more handsome man."

Paul glanced at Justice. "Well, I'm going to have to disagree."

"That's probably a good thing. It'd be weird if you were lusting after my mate." Oscar blanched. "Sorry. Again, there goes the mouth."

"It's okay. Do you want to have a seat, and maybe we can talk for a while?" Paul asked. "I can get us some glasses. I meant to bring them out in the first place, but…"

But he'd wanted an excuse to go in and get himself together if necessary. Justice had talked it over with him and frankly, Paul was doing so much better than either of them had expected.

"That'd be nice. When you get back, we can talk about what plans we're implementing here, and if you have any questions for Jo that would put you more at ease around him, please ask."

"Wow, Oscar, that sounded very mature and compassionate," Justice teased as Paul went inside. "I'm impressed."

Oscar flipped him off. "Be a shame if I tripped when I was pouring your glass of tea. Might end up getting you wet."

"Behave, sweetheart," Josiah told Oscar. "You're a little wired today."

"I've had about three hours' sleep all week, I'm brain-dead, not wired," Oscar retorted.

Paul returned holding a tray with iced glasses and fresh chocolate chip cookies on it. "Brought out the heavy-duty friendship-building food. Cookies."

"Home-made?" Oscar asked. "Oh, they are," he cooed as he plucked one off the tray. "Who baked these?"

"I did, last night." Justice held up his hand for a second then lowered it. "Because I am just that awesome."

"You really are," Paul said as Oscar groaned around a mouthful of cookie. "And you're all mine."

"Young love," Josiah sighed. "Or maybe that should be new love. Y'all are both older than Oscar."

Justice stilled on the inside, his senses pricking sharp then calming. He looked at Paul, who was staring at him with a rather shocked look on his face.

It was in that moment, as he gazed into Paul's eyes, that he realised he did love his mate. Not just liked, not just felt affection for, but the deep, abiding love he'd always hoped to have.

Justice couldn't hide it from Paul, either. He saw no reason to try. He let the feeling flow from him to his mate. Paul's eyes shimmered with tears, and his lips trembled.

"Maybe we should go —" Josiah began.

Justice waved him off. He cupped Paul's chin and gently kissed those quivering lips. He didn't mind anyone seeing him, knowing he was proclaiming his love to his mate with the kiss.

Or that Paul was proclaiming it right back, opening for him, trusting Justice to lead the kiss and keep him safe, not to abuse his strength. Justice drank in his mate's taste, the quiet, barely-there sob that Paul fed into him. He held Paul after the kiss ended, with Paul sitting beside him on the porch swing again, legs tucked under him and curled against Justice's side.

It was a peaceful visit, an easy, getting-to-know-one-another event that would always be one of Justice's favourite memories. The first time he ever fell in love, or better still, the only time he would ever fall in love, because it would last forever between him and Paul.

After an hour of visiting, Paul seemed comfortable, mostly, around Josiah. Justice didn't think he'd be asking the guy to play poker or anything any time soon, but the seeds of friendship had been planted.

"We'd better go. Remus and a slew of family are supposed to be arriving tonight and tomorrow." Oscar grinned at him. "It's like a whole 'nother family reunion for y'all since you didn't make the original one this year. Grandma Marybeth even mentioned making it a twice-yearly event so everyone can make it to one or the other, or both." Oscar stopped grinning so quickly it was like he'd slapped a mask on. "I've gotten better about the reunions, but I still don't like them."

"Aw, I think you do," Josiah teased. "Can't admit it, because people might think you have a soft heart."

Oscar gave his mate a narrow-eyed look. "I don't have a heart."

Josiah laughed and laughed until he had to bend over and hold his stomach. Justice wasn't the only one wondering if the man had slipped a rung on his mental ladder.

"Come on," Josiah gasped, his eyes crinkled with the size of his smile. "He's trying to be Billy Badass here, or Oscar—"

"Don't say it," Oscar warned in a low voice.

"The Grouch," Josiah continued, "And we all know he'd turn himself inside out for any one of his family or friends. He loves them all."

Oscar turned his nose up, but the corners of his mouth twitched as he hooked an arm through one of Josiah's. "I'll make you pay for spilling all of my secrets, mate."

"Promises like that just warm my willy," Josiah retorted.

Oscar scrunched up his nose as he looked at Josiah. Justice laughed and Paul snorted.

"Please don't ever use that phrase again," Oscar finally said. "Not if you ever hope to have your *dick* anywhere near me again."

Josiah saluted Oscar. "Turns me on when you get all bossy, you know."

"Which is only part of why I do it." Oscar waved at them then headed back to his place.

"They seemed kind of fun, actually," Paul said as he watched them walking away. "I like Oscar. He's not nice all the time. Makes me feel like less of a jerk, because I'm not nice all the time either."

"But I wouldn't have you any other way," Justice assured him. "I do love you, just as you are, and I'll keep loving you no matter how you might change."

Paul's eyes welled over and he hugged Justice so hard it knocked the breath right out of him. "I love you too. So much."

It was a better day than Justice had expected, and it'd already started off perfect with Paul giving him the best blow job. Justice had lost it there at the end, and Paul had eaten that right up.

Paul trusted him. Paul loved him. Things would only get better between them.

Chapter Fourteen

An annoying buzzing woke Paul up. He poked Justice's side. "S'your phone going off." It sounded like it was going to vibrate right off the nightstand. Justice snored and Paul jabbed him harder. "So much for shifters having superior hearing."

"I heard that," Justice slurred as he slapped at the stand. "You wore me out, honey."

Well, Paul couldn't complain about that. The last two sessions with Vivian had been intense, and he'd needed a lot of relief afterwards. That Justice getting off did more for Paul sometimes than coming himself came in handy.

Paul turned on the lamp by his side of the bed. "Maybe it's Oscar telling you everyone arrived," Paul said as Justice finally grabbed the phone. There'd been one delay after another, even for the much-anticipated arrival of Remus, the Super Shaman, as Paul was tending to think of him.

Justice sat up, suddenly alert. "No. No, it's not. I think it's a text from Cliff. How'd that fucker get my number?"

Paul tried not to give in to the fear that clutched at his heart. "Why do you think it's him?"

Justice fired off a text. "Because all it says is, 'Two more down, five to go. Your apartment wasn't clean in the first place—the blood will wash out. Maybe. C.' What the hell, man?"

"Two down? He killed two more?"

"Sounds like it," Justice said. "What was he doing in my apartment?"

"He knew." Paul wasn't tired at all now. "They know about me and you, obviously. I'd hoped it was only that…that Cliff guy, but either he told them or they knew somehow, and they went to your place looking for me—"

Justice's phone buzzed again. He read the message then glanced at Paul. "You're good. He broke into my place and waited. I don't think he told them about us."

Paul remembered something Justice had said in one of their conversations about Cliff. "He told you his goal is to protect his species. Don't you think someone like that wouldn't care about using me as bait?"

Justice set the phone down, frowning. "I don't know. I really don't know him, or what he's capable of doing. He has power, but I don't know anything about that, either. Now I wonder, whose side is he on?"

"The side of his people." Paul thought that was obvious. "What if he didn't hide away the other freed people? What if he killed them to keep everything about shifters a secret?"

Justice snapped his gaze to Paul's. "Gods, he could have. I just believed what he said. Fuck, I let him go."

"Which was for the best," Paul assured him. "We could be wrong, he might be the most honourable man in the world next to you. All I'm saying is, we don't know him. No one does." They'd found that out through the family gossip. Even Marybeth had been confounded by what she'd heard about Cliff.

"I need to go to Phoenix."

Paul shoved the covers off. "Okay, then let's go."

Justice shook his head. "No, you need to stay here. I don't want you with me in case Cliff is there."

The idea of that scared the shit out of Paul, but he wasn't going to let that keep him from being with Justice. "I'll set the Taser you got me on crispy. I'm not staying here without you."

"Paul, be reasonable," Justice began.

Which put 'reasonable' off the table and slammed 'pissed off' smack dab front and centre. "Be reasonable? *Reasonable?* How is leaving me here reasonable? Don't you think that if this was a plan to get your attention, maybe the goal is to get you away from me so I can be killed? Or you can, then me? Maybe you leaving me here plays right into their hands, whether 'they' is Cliff or the other fuckers who want me dead." He got up on his knees and scooted over to Justice. Logic was probably his best bet. "We need to stay together. If we're separated, and someone were to get one of us, they'd have the leverage to have us both, wouldn't they?"

"Yes," Justice agreed. He rubbed his hands over his face then pulled at his hair. The once-short strands had got long enough to be gripped. Justice did it hard enough that his eyebrows were tugged up, making him look like he'd had bad plastic surgery.

Justice let go of his hair and massaged his scalp. "Hate it when I do that. Stings."

"Then maybe you shouldn't pull it," Paul suggested. "How are we getting to Phoenix?"

"We'll drive," Justice said after a jaw-popping yawn. "I need to call Oscar, let him know what's going on. He can fill everyone else in. I want to get on the road."

Paul thought about suggesting they get more sleep, but knew that'd be futile. They were both wide awake. *Almost wide awake.* "I'm going to make some coffee."

"Make it strong enough to scoop out with a spoon," Justice said as Paul stumbled out of bed. "Like coffee porridge or something."

"Gross, but probably necessary." Paul started to make his way to the kitchen, only whacking his hip on the dresser as he tried to get his sweats on before he got out of the bedroom. Justice was already in the bathroom by then. The man was faster at waking up than Paul ever would be.

He still had the coffee done and a cup of it chugged down before Justice came in wearing black jeans and shirt.

"Looking to do a little breaking and entering?" Paul asked as he poured Justice a mug of coffee.

"This feels like it calls for blending in with the night." Justice took the cup and closed his eyes as he inhaled deeply. "Gods, Paul. If I weren't already in love with you, this would have done it."

"And then I would have always thought you only loved me for my coffee."

A knock at the door startled a squeak out of Paul. He slapped a hand over his mouth, not just from sheer mortification. Someone was outside and he didn't know who.

Justice gently pried his hand off his mouth and gave him a chaste kiss. "Oscar, and probably Josiah. I'll get the door."

"I'll pour the coffee." Paul's heart was racing. He pressed a hand to his chest, and Justice's soothing voice in his head helped calm him down. There was a lot going on, and he still had panic attacks. He wasn't healed up, and might not be for years, but he was getting better. He could do without all the new drama, but at least he had fabulous people around him.

He had a family, even if he might be a little nervous around some of them.

"What's going on?" he heard Oscar ask as soon as the door was opened. "Gawd, I need coffee."

"Coming right up," Paul called out.

"We'll come in the kitchen, honey," Justice told him. "Don't worry about bringing it out."

"Okay." Paul set the mugs on the table and took the half and half from the fridge. It'd do for creamer if anyone wanted some. The sugar was in the cabinet, and as he got that out, he kept an eye on the kitchen door. Justice came through first, with Oscar and Josiah right behind him.

There was the fluttering in his chest again, and the tight squeeze of his lungs. Paul grabbed the sugar and began the calming breathing he'd been working on. For all he knew, it wasn't even Josiah who was threatening to set off a panic attack. He'd just been feeling edgy and over-stressed. Coffee, though he needed the caffeine, probably hadn't been the best idea.

He brought the bag down right before Justice appeared beside him. *"It's okay, honey. Just take deep breaths, and focus on my voice."*

Paul did, and the panic attack died before it could truly grip him. Paul opened his eyes, having closed them to concentrate on his breathing technique. "Thanks."

Justice rubbed the small of his back. "Any time."

When Justice's fingers glanced over one of Paul's scars, Paul was reminded that he hadn't put a shirt on. He was only wearing sweat pants. His scars were horrible and there for everyone to see.

"You're beautiful," Justice told him. "If this will help you relax, take it." He pulled off his shirt, slipped the bag of sugar out of Paul's grasp and slid the shirt over Paul's head, saving him from having to run to the bedroom for clothing.

Paul turned and gave his man a proper kiss, with tongue and gratitude.

"Guys, coffee," Josiah whined. "Please? Pretty please?"

Paul stepped back, feeling much better than he had a few minutes ago. "Coffee," he said as he twisted around to grab the pot. "There's creamer on the table and Justice has the sugar. Grab spoons from the drawer on the right if you need one." Paul poured the coffee. There was something so relaxing about the deep, dark colour of coffee, and the scent—the only thing that smelt better was Justice.

There wasn't any talking until Oscar and Josiah had chugged their first cup. They both held their empties out to him, pleading silently with their eyes. Paul rolled his. "Aren't y'all family now? Which means self-serve?" But he grinned and poured the coffee, topping off Justice's cup last. "Let me get another pot going real quick. Commence plotting and planning."

They did, and Paul listened as Justice told them about the text message and their possible scenarios.

"He never texted back again?" Oscar asked.

"Not after that, no. You'd have to meet the guy, he's—" Justice paused. Paul finished preparing the coffee pot and pressed the button to get it brewing. "He's weird, yeah, but it's not just that. There's this…this power, that he exudes even though it seems like he's trying not to. I can't wrap my head around him being a bad guy, but I can believe he'd do anything necessary to protect shifters from being exposed to human beings." Justice looked at him. "Anything, and that's not acceptable."

"I wish Remus was here. How odd is it that some kind of sickness hits his pack when he was about to come out?" Oscar mused.

"At least it isn't deadly," Josiah added. "That's my family, too. So far it's only been headache and, uh, gastrointestinal issues. That's still something that we've never had to deal with before. Shit, shifters don't get sick."

"Unless humans pollute their environment with chemicals to treat weeds and make the soil better, or to take care of pests and rodents," Oscar griped. "It's not just our kind they're poisoning, or the weeds or bugs or whatever. The humans are getting sick, too."

Paul sat beside Justice. "How'd the shifters get exposed?"

Josiah grunted and crossed his arms over his chest as he glared off at some point in the distance. "Farmer nearby got careless, polluted the whole goddamned river. Maybe it wouldn't make a human so sick, but it's causing problems that Remus has been able to fix so far. The Fates are being good to us, but humans are trying to kill us even inadvertently."

"I'm sorry." Paul didn't hate all wolf shifters, apparently, because he really was sorry Josiah's pack family was suffering. "They'll be okay though?"

"Remus says they will, but the kids won't be able to go playing in the river like we did growing up. Not without the water being checked first." Josiah sighed and looked tired. "It seems like a piece of my youth just got poisoned." Then he smacked his forehead. "Damn, I sound like a whiny bastard. This is what happens when I don't get enough coffee in me."

Paul rose from his seat and got the fresh pot of coffee. "Let's cure that problem, at least." He began pouring everyone fresh coffee then sat down once he'd finished. He left the coffee pot sitting on the table. It wouldn't be there long enough to cool off.

"When's Remus coming here?" Justice asked.

Josiah hitched a shoulder. "I don't know now. Supposed to be here later today—" He looked at the clock. "It's almost four a.m., so he was supposed to be here in about twelve hours, but chances are someone else will get ill. Wasn't just the kids that played in the river. Lots of the adult shifters liked to go have fun in it at night."

"At least Bobby and Sully didn't get sick. Remus would probably end up dragging both of their whiny asses back to the river and drowning them. I remember when Sully hammered his thumb a few years ago. Could hear him whining all across Grandma's house." Oscar shook his head. "Can't imagine Bobby would be a good patient, either."

"Nah, he's a big baby," Josiah agreed.

"We've gotten off track," Justice said. "Not that I don't hope your pack will all recover, and the farmer will get locked up for environmental contamination or something. I do, but I want to get on the road."

"My fault. I started babbling about it all." Josiah waved a hand. "This Cliff guy, he helped Wes and his mate free a kid who was being held in one of those conversion camps. I think he killed a few people then. Not sure how what he was doing there helped out the shifter people."

Oscar made a humming sound before he spoke. "Yeah, I meant to tell you about that, Jus. Wes said Cliff helped because he'd been in conversion hell before. Maybe he doesn't just focus on helping shifters, if that's the truth."

Justice growled and twirled his coffee cup around on the table. "Damn it, I thought we could move him over into the bad guy side, but knowing that he helped Wes rescue a human? I don't know what to think anymore."

"I think it's best to err on the side of caution," Oscar said. "Don't trust him, but don't kill him on sight, either."

"That is generally the way I deal with most people," Justice said dryly. "We're going to pack a few days' worth of clothes and hit the road. If you hear anything, see anything suspicious, let me know. We'll do the same."

"Hopefully we'll just be cleaning up a mess someone else made." Paul repressed a shudder. He was afraid he would freak out over the blood, if there really was any.

"Be careful." Oscar and Josiah stood. Oscar clapped him on the back. "Don't let my cousin do anything stupid."

"Wouldn't dream of it." Paul awkwardly thumped Oscar's back in return. Josiah winked at him and Paul felt his cheeks warming with a blush.

After they left, Paul and Justice packed a few changes of clothes. Paul took his Taser out of the nightstand drawer. He hadn't practised with it, but he figured it wouldn't be too hard to work. At least he'd read the manual on it and watched the how-to video.

It took them another fifteen minutes until they were out of the door. Justice locked the place up then took Paul's hand. "We're going to be fine."

"I know." Being positive was half the victory. They walked to the car, and a familiar, unwelcome sensation slithered down Paul's spine. *"Justice."*

"I feel it. The wind's wrong. Can't scent anything out of the ordinary. Take my phone and text Oscar. It might be Levi or Lyndon out on patrol."

"Maybe." Paul lifted Justice's phone from his shirt pocket. He had the text sent before they reached the vehicle.

Justice unlocked the doors and opened Paul's. "After you."

It was cheesy, and sweet. Paul got in. He buckled up after Justice shut the door. Paul watched him walk around to the driver's side door. Justice got in and Paul breathed a sigh of relief. He'd halfway expected an attack.

"Here." He handed Justice his phone. Justice pushed it back towards him.

"You hold it. I won't be messing with it since I'm driving." He started the car.

Paul jumped when the phone vibrated. He read the message out loud. "'Levi and Lyndon are on the loose. Jo and I will shift and make sure no one else is out there. Go, we've got this'."

"Oscar has really grown up," Justice said as he put the car in gear. He began backing it up as he talked. "It's so weird trying to match up the memories I have of him as a kid hiding away from most of the family at the reunions. He's not shy or insecure now. Not at all."

"Wow, I can't imagine him being anything less than borderline dynamic. He doesn't seem to be the kind of person who would be intimidated by anyone."

They continued to talk for the first few hours of the trip. Eventually, Paul grew so sleepy that he nodded off despite his best attempts not to. When he woke up, it was because the change in the sound of the engine reached him through his sleep. He blinked and wiped away the bit of drool at the edge of his mouth. "Where are we?" The question came out slurred. Paul scrubbed at his eyes and yawned. "I need to fuel up and my bladder's not happy at all."

Justice exited the highway and drove to a busy-looking gas station. "You hungry?"

Paul arched his back, trying to work out a kink in it. "Nothing like gas station food to wake me up. Mmm, burnt grease."

Justice laughed and parked the car at a pump. "Well, if you don't want the grease, they have a Subway here. You could get us both a sandwich while I'm pumping gas and using the restroom."

"I'll do that, after I hit the restroom up first. What do you want on your sub?" Paul should have known Justice would want as much meat as he could get. Justice handed him thirty bucks. "Thanks."

Paul tucked the money into his front jeans pocket then headed in to use the restroom. He held his breath as long as he could as he pissed. The place was more on the nasty side than not, with suspiciously wet floors and no soap in the dispensers.

After tucking his cock away, and ignoring the other men draining their bladders, Paul washed his hands to the best of his ability. He remembered that he'd read somewhere twenty seconds of washing your hands under running water killed most germs. It'd have to do, either way. Paul shut the knob off with his elbow, shook his hands, then left the restroom, glad someone was coming in as he was going out so he didn't have to touch the door handle.

Subway had a line, but it moved quickly. Justice joined him before their sandwiches were made, though. Paul couldn't help it, he was smiling like a loon just because Justice was there with him.

They took their food and drinks back to the car. "You won't text and drive, but you're going to eat and drive?" Paul asked.

Justice started the car. "No, I'm going to park the car, leave it running and eat this sandwich of the gods. Then I'll drive."

"I can drive," Paul offered. "I had a nap. I promise not to run off the road or anything. I do—I did have a license. It wouldn't have expired yet."

Justice gave him a soft look and he stroked Paul's cheek. "You can drive. I trust you."

After Justice parked the car again, Paul ate half of his sub and folded the wrapper around the other half for later. Justice finished soon after, and they swapped seats. Paul adjusted the seat and mirrors. "Back on the highway we exited?"

"Yeah." Justice leaned his seat back and closed his eyes. "Gonna be on it for about three hundred miles. Exit one eighty-two."

"Got it."

Justice was asleep before they got out of the parking lot.

It had been almost two years since Paul had driven. He was nervous at first, but the thrill of the freedom soon chased away his nerves. He wasn't driving a fancy car, but he didn't care. It just felt good to hold that steering wheel in his hands and take on the open highway.

Dust devils tore up the land on either side of them off and on. Paul would have loved to have watched them, but he was maxing out the speed limit. Another time, he promised himself.

When he saw the exit he was supposed to take, Paul was surprised. Time had flown faster than the car's tires on the asphalt.

"Hey, Justice, I'm taking that exit."

Justice huffed, waking up unwillingly it seemed, but by the time they were on the next stretch of road, he was awake, if not fully alert.

"Still got about six hours or so to go," Justice said. "I'm about hungry again."

"Eat the rest of my sandwich, if you want. Maybe it'll tide you over for an hour or two until there's somewhere decent to stop."

The trip was fun, even though Paul was worried about what they'd find once they entered Justice's apartment. That fear made him treasure every minute he spent laughing and talking with Justice even more.

A little over thirteen hours after they'd left, Justice parked the car in the lot at his apartment complex. "I'm not parking close to where my place is, just in case someone's watching it. My ass is asleep."

"I'll wake it up first chance I get," Paul promised. "Do you think maybe we should wait until it gets dark?"

"I'd rather not. That'd be more dangerous for us, I think," Justice explained. "There's a couple of ball caps in our duffle. They aren't much of a disguise, but they're still better than nothing."

Paul turned around after he unbuckled. He leaned over the seat and opened the duffle. He retrieved the two caps and sat back down. "You pick first."

Justice took the black one with silver stitching. Paul put the dark blue one on his head. "Let's go."

Chapter Fifteen

After weeks in the country, breathing in pure mountain air, the scents of the city were an affront to Justice's nasal passages. His nose itched, twitched and burned. "Damn it."

"What's wrong?" Paul asked as they strode towards the sidewalk that wound around the sprawling apartment complex.

"I'm getting congested. This shit never happened when I was a kid, but maybe Oscar and Josiah are on to something. So many more pollutants around nowadays." He pinched his nose to ward off a sneezing fit. Then his eyes started to water. "Fugh." Justice stopped them in the shade.

Paul giggled nervously.

Justice blinked then stopped pinching his nose so he could swipe at his eyes. It took him a few minutes, but he got his body under control. Unfortunately, that didn't include his sense of smell.

"I can't scent like I'm usually able to," Justice grumbled. "Damn it, I grew up here, lived here until I joined the Marines, then moved back. I've never had allergies."

Paul cocked his head and considered Justice. "I have, and nothing's bothering me here."

They both stared at each other, wariness creeping back and forth between them. Paul finally spoke. "As sensitive as your nose is, I wouldn't necessarily be bothered by the same chemicals or smells that you would. I wouldn't even be aware of them."

Justice pinched his nose again, but the sneeze slammed into him anyway and he let go before his ears popped or his eyes bugged out.

"Bless you," Paul murmured. "Maybe it is some kind of allergy. After all, people develop allergies after being exposed to something, right?"

"I don't know, but whatever it is, it sucks ass." He sniffled and tipped his head back. "I don't get the feeling we're being watched."

"That's good," a deep, rough and familiar voice said.

Paul's freckles stood out in stark relief as he paled, his eyes settling on the big man Justice turned to find behind him.

Justice backed away until he was standing with his back pressed to Paul's front. "What are you doing here, Cliff?"

Paul began to shake.

Cliff arched a bushy brow. "Thought maybe he'd gotten past being scared of wolf shifters."

"What are you doing here?" Justice repeated. He reached behind him and Paul gripped his hand.

Cliff moved back a few steps and Justice thought regret flashed over his features before aloofness took its place. "I actually felt bad about the blood stains. I figured that was something your mate didn't need to see."

Paul's breathing was too fast, too rough. Justice silently tried to soothe him as he kept his gaze locked on Cliff. "So you were just doing something nice."

Cliff shrugged. "It happens. Just not to me. I didn't want there to be any traces of death left behind in case the cops showed up. I assure you, it was all self-serving on my part." Cliff pulled the leather necklace out from beneath his shirt. He held it right above the little jar hanging on it.

Paul's wheezing was loud, his panic palpable.

Then Cliff closed his eyes and gripped that container in his hand. Silver light slipped out from between his fingers as he spoke words that Justice didn't understand. They weren't English, yet something deep inside him responded, his leopard wanting out to bow at Cliff's feet.

His leopard was obviously suffering from some kind of head trauma.

Cliff opened his eyes. The gold and silver irises seemed to glow for one second, then Cliff blinked and let go of the necklace. He turned and waved as he walked off.

"What the—" Justice spun around. Paul was staring open-mouthed at Cliff as he walked away. "Paul?"

Paul closed his mouth only long enough to swallow. "It stopped. The panic attack, it was a bad one. He scared me, Justice. He's...there's something about him that just seems so big and powerful. I couldn't breathe, I couldn't calm down, and he started that chanting. Everything just calmed inside me."

Justice wanted to pull Paul close and hold him, kiss him, but had to restrain himself until they were inside his apartment. He settled for cupping Paul's elbow and steering him in the right direction.

"I really don't know what to make of him," he confided in Paul. "I was more than halfway convinced he was an enemy, then Oscar talked me into reserving judgement, and now he did some kind of shamanistic voodoo on you."

Paul gave him a sideways look. "Why do you think it's any kind of voodoo? Or were you joking?"

"Joking, mainly. I do think he has some kind of shaman powers, although I thought shamans were healers, not killers." Justice sniffed. He still couldn't catch more than the basic scent of his surroundings. Why hadn't whatever Cliff done helped him out any?

By the time they'd taken the circuitous route to his second floor apartment, the Phoenix sun had worked them both into a sweat. Justice could smell man, and arousal, his mate turned on by him for no other reason than that he was there. It was hot as hell to be able to affect someone so. Paul did it for him like that.

Justice took the keys out of his pocket. He kept Paul behind him just in case. Just in case what, he wasn't sure, but if there was something or someone waiting to kill them, he was going to do everything he could to protect Paul.

Paul stayed close behind him as Justice unlocked the door. There were two deadbolts and the knob itself to unlock. He wondered how Cliff had got inside.

"Maybe he used some of that shamanistic voodoo," Paul offered.

"It's possible." Justice didn't bother to keep the thought unspoken. If anyone was inside, they'd know he was coming from all the tumblers being tipped.

He opened the door and the first thing he noticed was the nose-searing scent of bleach. "Fuck, what'd he do, soak everything in that shit?"

Paul nudged him, trying to get inside. "What? I don't smell anything."

Justice exhaled through his nose, trying to get the stench out. "Bleach. You can't smell any of it?" he asked as he entered the living room. Paul followed him. Justice closed and locked the door. He held up a finger and quietly began checking the place out. Paul stayed by him, a quiet shadow with a Taser in his hands. Justice hadn't even realised Paul had tucked it in his baggy shorts.

Knowing Paul hadn't practised with the Taser made Justice a tad jumpy about having Paul at his back. He knew Paul wouldn't hurt him on purpose, but even a stumble could end with Justice being Tasered.

The place was cleaner than he and Viv had left it. After inspecting every room, he leaned against the living room wall and pulled Paul to him. "Cliff must have some issues. All of our dirty laundry's been washed, dried, folded, ironed, hung up. Those sheets on my bed? Never seen 'em before, but they're nice ones, I'd bet. There's food in the pantry, too. New rug on the—"

"Yeah, that's better than what I thought we'd find." Paul wiggled until he was plastered to Justice's front. Paul's erection just about burned a trail on Justice's thigh as Paul began to slowly rut against him.

Justice forgot about his nose and bent to kiss Paul's parted lips. The taste of Paul was better than anything he'd ever imagined. It rocked him every time they kissed.

"Should let me ditch this Taser so we can get naked in your big bed," Paul said against his lips.

Justice thought that sounded great, right after another kiss or three. He looped his arms around Paul's shoulders and dipped down for more kisses.

Paul played dirty, thank the gods, reaching between them and getting a handful of Justice's dangly bits. When Paul began backing away, Justice followed him, closely. They made it to the bedroom and Paul set the Taser down on the floor beside the bed.

"Strip," Paul ordered.

Justice started to, then his heart must have completely stopped beating as he saw the tiny red light showing through the gauzy curtains. He yelled, panic hitting him so hard his strength just about left him. Just about, but didn't, not until he'd tackled his startled mate, taking him down in a leap that was none too gentle. The sound registered then—glass being penetrated by the sharp metal, the bullet ripping through the air. There was no implosion, explosion, no loud firing of a weapon. *Silencer,* Justice thought.

Justice couldn't say how it happened, whether he'd heard the muted sounds first or whether he'd taken Paul down first. His ears were ringing, and people were going to be calling the cops. His shoulder ached like a mother, too, and Justice groaned as he rolled them, never being still. They went off the bed, then Justice shoved Paul hard, pushing him under the bed frame.

"Justice," Paul hissed. "Your shoulder!"

He guessed he knew why it hurt. The bullet must have hit him, or winged him, something. If he'd been hit, it wasn't a bad wound. It wasn't like he was dizzy or… He blinked, trying to clear away the multitude of grey and black spots cluttering his vision.

* * * *

Paul bit his tongue to keep from screaming out Justice's name. He didn't think the wound was that bad, but maybe Justice had been shot somewhere other than the very top of his shoulder?

Now wasn't the time for him to look. Paul grabbed Justice's arms. "Don't you pass out on me, you big lug. I need you to stay awake and help me stay safe. Come on, roll under here with me." He didn't hear any more of the odd sound the shot had made, but that didn't mean they were out of the woods yet. "Justice!" Paul snapped in as loud a voice as he dared.

Justice moaned and opened dazed eyes to look at him.

"Come on, under the bed," Paul repeated.

Justice shuffled alongside of him, hissing every few seconds. Paul felt along his back as best he could. The only wound he found was the one on the shoulder.

Then he heard the most terrifying sound he could imagine. The tumbling of the door locks.

"Fuck, no," Paul whispered, panic bleeding bright into his veins. "No. No! We're not dying here. Not letting them win." He refused to give in to the panic. If he did, whoever was coming through that door would kill them both.

Paul scurried out from under the bed, his eyes on the Taser. He could do it, he could save himself and Justice—as long as there was only a single person coming in.

It was the best he could do. Paul picked the thing up and held it in his hands. He played the video's main how-to's in his head as he stepped into the hallway. Whoever was picking the locks was beyond a fool. For all they knew, Paul could be waiting for them with a Taser—or a gun.

But if they'd seen the blood, and seen him and Justice, especially Justice, go down, then the shooter might not give a damn, because he wouldn't think Paul was a threat.

Paul was more than a threat. He was a fucking promise of retribution.

He was off to the side, almost behind the door, when it was opened. He had the Taser up, the setting on the highest one possible, and his aim was perfect. The shifter who came in had his back to Paul, but there was something familiar about him. He had a gun of some kind in his hands. Paul didn't know shit about guns, but it looked fancy and deadly.

The shifter shut the door and started to turn. As soon as Paul saw that hooked nose, he was thrown back to the worst of his wounds, his most humiliatingly given one.

He pressed the button of the Taser, shouting, "Fuck you!" as he did so.

The look of surprise on the wolf shifter's face was classic as the Taser hit him and sent electrical currents into him.

Keep moving, don't stand there and watch, that was the advice in the video, or some of it. Paul darted to the kitchen. He grabbed the largest knife he could find from the knife block as he watched the wolf squirm on the ground.

Wolves must have been high-stun proof, though. The man was already pulling at the Taser wires and cursing when Paul started for him.

"You'll pay, pet," the nasty shifter said, eyes gleaming with a sadistic streak Paul would never understand. "Don't you know, didn't you learn anything all the times I fucked you? Wolf shifters are tougher than anyone else—"

Paul growled, fury and memories making him braver than he'd thought to be. "Shut up and die, asshole."

The man looked surprised, then he cackled and began to get to his feet. His gun had landed a half dozen feet away, under the couch. "I'm going to enjoy teaching you a lesson again before I kill you, pet."

Paul would die before the fucker ever got any pleasure from him. He feinted to the left and the man almost fell over trying to avoid being stabbed. Paul grinned. His foe wasn't so steady, despite his words.

Paul stabbed and jabbed rapidly, trying to keep the movements random. He wanted the asshole dead, not carved up, but it was looking like that would be all he could manage.

Then a large figure appeared behind the man. Paul only had a second to figure out that it was Cliff before the other shifter was grabbed and practically thrown on his knife.

It sank deep into the man's chest. A sickening suctioning noise slipped from his mouth as it dropped open. Blood trickled from the corner of his mouth while more ran thickly from the knife wound.

Cliff closed the door as the last bit of life drained from the man's eyes.

"Sorry about that." Cliff tipped his chin at the dead body. "And I just replaced the damned rugs. Stop looking at the dead guy, Paul. It'll just keep freaking you out."

"Justice—" Paul began, but Cliff sighed like he was vexed.

"He's a wuss." Cliff locked the locks. He stepped over the dead man and started for the bedroom.

"Wait!" Paul still wasn't sure that Cliff could be trusted.

Cliff kept walking. "If I'd wanted him or you dead, we wouldn't be having this moment in time together."

The guy was a prick. That was all there was to it. Paul had just killed someone—well, no, he hadn't. He'd been trying, but it had been Cliff who'd tossed the other shifter onto the knife.

"Justice," was all Cliff said as he entered the bedroom. He took something out of the little jar and bent to peer under the bed. "Oh good, he's unconscious. That will make this so much easier. Shit tastes disgusting."

"What are you doing?" Paul asked hurriedly as he got down on the floor.

"Fixing him," Cliff replied. "I have my shamanistic voodoo shit down, baby."

Paul froze. How had Cliff known that was what they'd called his…his shamanistic stuff?

Cliff moved back and hauled Justice out from under the bed. "All right, he needs to be cleaned off. It's just a flesh wound, nothing major. It's the poison that was on it that's giving him fits."

"Poison?" Paul scrambled to his feet as Cliff rose and swooped Justice into his arms like the man weighed nothing. "He's going to be all right, right? Tell me he'll be all right!"

"Course he will," Cliff assured him as he plopped Justice down in the tub. "Now you take care of your mate here, and I'm going to go clean up that goddamned mess. Again. Hey, four to go."

Paul didn't care, not right then. He struggled to get Justice undressed and the blood cleaned off him. The wound really was shallow, but the poison—Paul wondered what kind it was.

He got the worse of the blood rinsed away. Whatever Cliff had given Justice, it seemed to be helping. Justice was breathing deeply, steadily, and he had good colour to his skin. Paul tried to get him out of the tub, but he couldn't manage it. Cliff came back in and lifted Justice for him.

Paul didn't care for seeing his mate—naked, wet, gorgeous—in another man's arms.

"Chill, he ain't my type, kiddo," Cliff told him as he gently settled Justice onto the bed. "I need to get back to the cleaning. You two have fun."

* * * *

Hours later, Paul woke up. He hadn't meant to fall asleep. Justice snored softly beside him. Paul checked his brow and found it nice and cool, like Paul's own. Then he looked at the wound where the bullet had struck and gasped to find it already healed over with pink skin.

When Paul could finally prise himself away from his mate, he quietly sneaked out of the bedroom. The apartment had a strangely empty feel to it, which was ridiculous because Justice was there with him. It didn't surprise him to find that Cliff had left. It was creepy, a little, but Paul was too tired to worry about that.

The living room looked as if it could be in some fancy magazine. There was no blood, no gore, no Taser parts or guns by the door. It was as if there had never been a violent confrontation, and death, in the room only hours ago.

More of Cliff's weird shamanistic voodoo. Somehow it didn't seem funny at all. It was scary—the man himself was scary. Paul hoped he never got on the man's bad side. Anyone who could heal up a wound so that it was just a pink scar? That was a formidable person you never wanted to piss off.

He heard the annoying buzz of Justice's phone and groaned when it dawned on him that they'd never let Oscar and the others know they'd arrived. He and Justice were both going to be in deep shit.

Paul took two bottles of water out of the fridge then he went to find the phone. It was under the bed, of course. He put the bottles on the nightstand then got down on hands and knees to retrieve the phone. There were several missed calls—Justice had set those to silent, he guessed—and a dozen texts.

They were *so* in trouble.

Or maybe not. He'd start with the good news that they were both okay, and Justice had survived being shot and poisoned. Paul was fairly certain those last two things were justifiable reasons for why neither he nor Justice had contacted the family.

He didn't want to try to text the whole thing to everyone, or one person then copy and paste that on, and on, and on. Paul knew just who he was going to call. Vivian. She had the right to know first.

Vivian answered on the second ring. "Hey, Paul, what's up? Is this a personal or a professional call?"

"Personal," he decided. "And not just for me. Is your family in Phoenix nearby?"

"Yes, they are, why?"

Paul began talking. Before he was off the phone with her, a knock sounded at the door.

"That's going to be our brother Joel and our parents," Vivian told him. "Joel's on the phone with Oscar. It's safe to open the door."

Paul still looked out of the peephole. There was no doubt that the people out there were Justice's family.

Not the woman and the younger man, at least. They looked almost like carbon copies of Justice.

"I've got it, Vivian. Do you want to stay on the phone with me?" Paul asked.

"Do you need me to?" Vivian asked in return. "Are you feeling okay?"

He was, surprisingly. Maybe he should have been nervous about meeting Justice's parents and brother, but he was more relieved that Justice was going to be okay than anything else.

"Thanks, Vivian. Love you."

Vivian sighed. "Aw, I love you too, Paul. You're my favourite brother, but don't tell the others."

After swearing that he wouldn't, he ended the call and began unlocking locks. In the back of his mind, he knew that there were probably some guidelines or rules that would make it necessary for Vivian to quit officially being his therapist now. As long as she was willing, and it was helping him, he didn't think they should stop.

Paul opened the door and damned his fair skin as he felt the blush start in. "Hi, come in," he said as he waved towards the living room.

Justice's mother entered first. She stopped in front of him and looked him over. Paul knew he wasn't anything special, and he had close to an inch of roots growing out from his bleach job. He looked a mess.

But she smiled and he was hugged quickly but firmly. "So you're my son's mate. It's good to meet you. Where is my baby?"

"Bedroom, sleeping," Paul told her. "Thank you."

"I'm Emily, by the way. You can call me Mom." And she was off to check on her son.

"I'm Lew," said the older, burly blond man who took Emily's — *Mom's* — place.

"Paul Hardy," Paul offered as he shook the man's hand. "You have a fantastic son."

"Thank you. We like him, most of the time," Lew said, giving him a wink. "Now Joel, here, sometimes we want to trade him in."

Joel laughed and swatted at his dad's arm. "Right, because my awesomeness makes the rest of you look bad."

"Say that to your mom." Lew shook his head. "Nah, don't. She'd have both our hides for joking like that."

Joel came in too, and introduced himself almost properly. He seemed to be a jokester, but other than that, Paul couldn't get a read on him. "Do y'all want to go check on Justice while I fix us some coffee? Or do you want tea, water, soda?"

"Coffee's good," Lew answered, "And we're fine on the couch. I hear Justice and Em coming this way."

Paul heard them then, too, the low rumble of Justice's voice and Emily's lighter, concerned one.

Paul went to the hallway and smiled so big his cheeks ached a little when he saw Justice walking with his arm around his mama. "Hey. How do you feel?"

Justice's smile was every bit as big as Paul's. "Man, I feel a lot better than I did when I crawled under the bed. What happened?"

"Cliff happened," Paul said. "Let me get some drinks together, then I'll explain to everyone." But he was already opening his mind, letting Justice see what had gone down when he'd been hurt.

"I'll help you," Emily — *Mom, I have to remember that or risk hurting her feelings* — offered.

They chatted pleasantly enough while Paul made the coffee and she started the water to brew some tea. Justice came in after greeting his dad and brother, and Paul couldn't help but be relieved. Mom seemed nice and all, but he was out of his element, or at least that was how he felt. Grandma Marybeth had been intimidating, too. He wondered how much scarring he had from his parents ditching him and Preston. Getting cosy with Lew didn't sound fun, either.

"We don't bite," Emily said as she steeped a couple of tea bags. Paul couldn't help but look at Justice, who was watching him with concern. Paul took a steadying breath and plastered on a smile.

"Yes, ma'am." He knew she hadn't meant to dredge up those bad memories.

"Ma'am?" Emily looked at him, one finely plucked brow arching perfectly. "Did you really just ma'am me?"

Paul started stuttering, trying to find the right answer to that.

"Leave him alone, Mom. Don't pick on my man." Justice stood and walked over to loop an arm around Paul's shoulder. "He's not used to decent parents."

A soft look settled on her features. "Oh. Well then. We'll just have to fix that, won't we?"

Justice nuzzled his cheek. *"How are you, seriously? You — Cliff pushed that guy and — "*

"I'm fine with it," Paul silently assured Justice. *"Maybe there should be some regret, but I don't feel any. If that makes me a bad person, whatever. That shifter was the one, the worst of them. I'm glad he's dead."*

"Me too, and I'm glad you're not upset. He isn't worth that kind of emotion."

"Boys, those silent mental conversations can be as rude as whispering in a roomful of people. Now, I don't mind, but some would kick up a fuss," Emily informed them. "Help me carry the drinks."

They did, and Paul sat on the arm of the chair Justice sprawled in. He mostly listened as everyone else talked. Every now and then, his gaze drifted to the pink scar on Justice's shoulder. It was close to where Paul liked to bite his mate. Maybe he should switch sides. The scar looked smaller already. It was unsettling how Cliff had done that.

Well, he didn't know how Cliff had done that. *With some words and herbs?* It was unsettling that he'd been able to do that, Paul corrected.

"We'll leave you to get some rest," Emily said sometime later as she stood. "Call if you need anything. Any idea how long y'all will be in town?"

Justice shrugged. "It's up to Paul. Obviously, the shifters who are after him know about me and him, and know where this place is. Or at least, some of them did."

"They have to know about your grandma's place, too," Lew pointed out. "That Cliff guy did. It wouldn't be hard for them to find out if they hadn't yet, either."

"Yeah, that's true," Justice agreed, "but it's easier to dispose of bodies in the woods, isn't it? And no one is going to call 911 because they heard fighting out at Grandma's. I think it's best to stay there until this is over."

"Good thinking, son," Lew said as he patted Justice's back. "I'll send a couple of your brothers out there, too. Give Marybeth more targets to pick on."

"I have to work," Joel stated firmly. "Can't take time off."

"I bet you can," Lew countered. "Your boss Clive is my best friend. Pretty sure he'd let you do your work like those telecommuters or whatever they're called."

Joel groaned and shortly thereafter, Paul and Justice were alone. Justice yawned and reached for him. "Bed?"

"Yeah." They went back into the bedroom. Paul looked around by the window. There was still a hole in it, but other than that, there were no signs of the shooting. Not even a trace of blood on the carpet.

"That's fucking creepy," he muttered.

"What is?" Justice sat on the bed and watched him.

"To know that Cliff was in here while we were sleeping. He cleaned up the blood." Paul shivered and turned away from the window. "I really hope he isn't a bad guy. He's got way too much power to be on the wrong side."

"No kidding. You want to head back tomorrow?" Justice asked. "I'd like to vacate as soon as possible."

"Whatever you want, I'm good with it." Paul eyed Justice's sexy body and leered.

Justice chuckled and lay back on the bed. "I wouldn't turn down a blow job."

Paul was more than all right with that.

Chapter Sixteen

Two to go.

Justice looked at the text. "He's got two left. I wonder if he's lying."

Paul rolled over and propped his head up on one fist. "I doubt it. Why would he?"

"Why does he text me this shit?" Justice retorted. "I mean, if he doesn't care about anything other than his own kind, why do this? Because I think he's sending the messages for you, honestly."

"So do I," Paul admitted. "I thought we'd kind of agreed that he's not as species-centric as he claimed."

Justice grunted and put the phone down. He waggled his eyebrows at Paul. "I seem to recall someone not getting off when I did."

Paul's cheeks blushed prettily as he licked his lips. "Yeah, about that…"

"About it, what? Is there something specific you want?" Justice asked his mate, stymied by the hesitation on Paul's part.

Paul licked his lips again and brought his gaze to Justice's. "Remember how we talked about trying the bite without sex?"

Fuck. Justice's dick went hard as stone immediately and his leopard mewled, begging for the chance to mark his mate. "Er, the problem is, I don't think I can do it and not have a hard-on. I might even come just from biting you. My leopard is really wanting to make you ours, but we don't have to." He rushed out the last five words.

Paul considered that for a few minutes before nodding awkwardly. "Okay, I think I'm okay with that. As long as we're not having sex when you do it, I probably won't freak out."

"Probably?" Justice squeaked. "I don't know—"

"Just do it," Paul snapped. "I'm so fucking tired of us having to hold back on things we want." Paul rolled onto his back and arched his neck. "Come on. I can feel how bad you want it."

Justice couldn't help but notice that Paul's cock was rising, pushing against the sheets. He'd love to touch it, stroke Paul off while marking him, but that wasn't on the table. *Yet.*

"I love you," Justice said as he moved closer. He bent his knees so he couldn't give in to the urge to rub against Paul's body. It made everything too uncomfortable position-wise. Justice flopped onto his back then stuffed a few of the pillows beneath his shoulders and head, propping him up to a goodly height. "How about this? You get on top, that way you control what happens? I'll even keep my hands on the headboard."

"I—" Paul swallowed twice, his Adam's apple bobbing enticingly. "Okay, yeah. I love you too,

Justice, and I think maybe I'd like your hands on me. My arms, or hips? Not holding, just touching me."

"I can so do that." Justice made sure the sheet was covering his rigid cock. He kept from reaching for Paul, letting his mate get settled astride him on his own terms.

Paul blushed furiously as he glared at his own pre-cum-beaded dick. "It's so messed up. I'm scared and so horny I'm dizzy."

"You have complete control of this," Justice assured him. "Any time at all that you want me to stop, I will. It's going to hurt, though. There's no way a bite can't be painful, but the pleasure…" He trailed off. Paul would have to decide if it was worth the trade-off.

Paul did so quickly, lowering himself down until his neck and shoulder were close to Justice's mouth. "Please," Paul asked in a quivering voice.

Fear and desire rolled off him in waves that Justice could sense even without their mental link. He gently stroked Paul's biceps, then leaned up a little and licked over the perfect spot to bite.

Paul whimpered and shook for him, chasing his mouth when Justice pulled back. The kiss was fierce and heady, with Paul demanding more from Justice than he ever had.

Justice gave it to him, moving his head aside to drag his chin along Paul's jaw, down his neck. He let his stubble abrade the skin there just a bit, drawing raspy moans from Paul.

Justice kept caressing his mate, and he felt it when Paul began to tremble and rock against him. The sharp jab of Paul's cock against his belly was so arousing he almost came then.

There was more, more that he wanted first. Justice urged Paul to come down more, to show that he truly wanted what would happen next.

Paul laid on him almost completely, only propping his shoulder and head up so Justice could get to that sweet spot. Justice rumbled his approval and opened his mouth and mind simultaneously, filling Paul with all the love, respect and need within him. At the same time, he bit, not dragging it out. His canines had dropped when Paul had asked about the bite in the first place.

Paul's blood held a sweet flavour to it. Justice sucked and moaned while Paul gasped and began thrusting wildly. Paul unravelled for him, coming in hot spurts that filled the room with the scent of his pleasure.

Justice couldn't hold back. His own cock pulsed, untouched for the most part, save the occasional rub of Paul's legs. Justice left off biting, lapping at the spot as he was turned inside out by ecstasy.

"Justice," Paul whispered before he let himself lie fully on Justice.

There was never so perfect a moment, Justice decided as he held his mate close.

* * * *

"I'd like to see Phoenix properly sometime. When we move back, after this is all over, I guess." Paul tapped out a beat along with the song on the radio.

Justice set the cruise control and relaxed in his seat. "I really do like my hometown, but it's not for everybody. If you decide you hate it, we'll go somewhere else."

"I like what I've met of your family there so far." Paul hadn't realised how badly he wanted to be a part of a family until he'd arrived at Marybeth's. Not right off the bat, but once he'd got past his submersion into his own misery.

"They're great," Justice assured him. "You'll love them, and they'll love you."

Justice's phone buzzed. Paul rolled his eyes. "I should get another cell phone. Maybe then I'd be getting texts from strange men."

Justice eyed him unhappily. "I think you need a cell phone, but the strange men part is questionable. What happened to your cell?"

Paul took Justice's phone from the centre console. "I accidentally threw it against the wall."

"Accidentally?"

Paul couldn't have missed that scepticism if he'd tried. "I don't even remember doing it, really. I freaked out I guess. Preston said I flung it then panicked. I think it was the other way around, probably. I was so scared, and my life was spinning out of control. I was pushing it out of control. Preston brought me to a place filled with strangers who I should have been terrified of, but they were nice and man, my head was a mess. I think I'm getting better though." He grinned as he touched the place where Justice had marked him. "This makes me horny every time I think about it."

"Me too," Justice said. "Me, you, whoever's doing the biting or getting bitten, it doesn't matter. It just makes my dick so hard I think I'm gonna die if I don't get some relief."

Paul noted the erection pushing at Justice's fly. "Too bad a blow job would be such a dangerous distraction."

Justice groaned and pressed a hand to his dick. "You're so mean. I'm going to have a hard-on until we can stop somewhere and I can beat off."

"No beating off," Paul told him. "I definitely want to blow you."

Justice cursed and Paul chuckled. He would make it worth Justice's wait. "Oh, shit. The phone." He'd forgotten he was even holding it. Paul clicked the button and unlocked the phone. "It's from Oscar. He said Remus is finally there, and wow, eleven more family members? Plus Remus brought some of his family." Paul closed his eyes, telling himself not to panic. "So there'll be more wolf shifters there."

"Good ones," Justice stressed. "Remember that."

"I'll try. He also says this Remus guy wants to meet with us, I mean, me. I wonder why." Paul's stomach kind of went all queasy on him upon reading that.

"He's a shaman, and he's a wolf shifter. He knows what happened to you. He will want to help you, if he can." Justice reached over and put his hand on Paul's thigh. "It's in his nature. He's supposed to be powerful, maybe even more than Cliff, so I don't think you'll panic with him."

"God, I hope not," Paul grumbled. "I'm so fucking tired of panic attacks. They have gotten better, though."

Justice squeezed his leg. "They have. So try not to worry about Remus and his pack members. It's going to be okay."

"Okay." Paul texted that one word back to Oscar. He didn't want to discuss it any more.

The thirteen-hour trip had them arriving back at Marybeth's in the early morning hours. Paul and Justice made a beeline for their cabin. Paul saw that tents had been put up all over the property. More than one had someone peeking out at their car as they drove to their place.

"This is weird," Paul said. "They're watching us."

"Watching out for us, too, remember." Justice turned to park beside their cabin. "They won't bother us. It does look like some kind of travelling caravan took over Grandma's property, though."

They got out, Paul grabbing the duffle and phone. No one approached them as they made their way up onto the porch, but once they were inside, Paul's mouth began to water.

"Grandma left us dinner," Justice said. "Yes!" He sprang up onto his toes. "Gods, I love my grandma!"

Paul thought if the food tasted half as good as it smelt, he'd love the woman too.

It was better. Paul moaned around a mouthful of homemade mashed potatoes and gravy.

"S'good," Justice got out before he shovelled a forkful of potpie in his mouth. "Guh."

That was the extent of their conversation. The food was too good to savour at first, but gradually, they slowed down until finally they had to quit eating.

"God, I'm stuffed," Paul whined, flopping back in his chair. "Can we just sleep here?"

"I was going to lick your balls and cock until you came once we got to bed, but if you'd rather stay here…"

Paul was up so quick he knocked his chair over. "After you," he said to Justice.

Justice gave him a half-grin. "Have to put up the leftovers first."

"You're a cruel man, but I love you." Paul helped Justice put everything away and rinse the dishes. They eyed each other hungrily once that was done and Paul sauntered over to his man. "Now, take me to bed."

Justice did, right after he kissed Paul breathless.

In the bedroom, he stripped Paul's clothes off, kissing over his bared skin. Justice gently pushed him back on the bed. Paul reached for his own nipples as Justice spread his legs.

"So sexy," Justice whispered, his breath tickling Paul's nuts.

Then the hot, wet swipe of tongue put an end to the tickling. Paul left off twisting his tits to instead pull his legs up, offering Justice more of him than he ever had.

"Paul?" Justice's voice was soft, holding a note of uncertainty.

"Please," Paul got out. "Let me feel your tongue."

There had been a time when he wouldn't have been so vague, but he was a different man now. A better one, he hoped. Paul's eyes rolled back when he felt that first, bare slide of tongue over his hole. He gripped his legs tighter, so tight it kind of hurt. Paul didn't care.

Justice lifted his balls, palming them as he began licking Paul's opening with more enthusiasm. The sounds he started making matched the hungry ones slipping past Paul's lips. Electric currents of pleasure spread from Paul's asshole to his cock and balls, then up to his nipples and down to his toes.

His head was definitely spinny, his breaths choppy as Justice rimmed him. When Justice gently sucked at that wrinkled skin, Paul yelped, his climax shoving at him. Justice rolled his balls and Paul let go of one leg to grab his dick. He didn't even make it before he started to come. Justice licked him, hard, rough, wet, and Paul keened as his cock spurted cum onto his belly.

Justice shook the whole bed as he rutted against the mattress. His shout when he came burst against Paul's delicate skin. It caused another dribble of cum to leak from his slit. Justice left off rimming him and sucked on one of Paul's nuts, sharing the happy orgasmic vibrations as he moaned through his release.

Once Paul could think, he was surprised he didn't soar off the bed from the sheer joy of being able to open himself up like he had to Justice.

He opened his arms to the man, and Justice crawled up Paul's body to nuzzle his neck.

Paul closed his eyes and enjoyed the sensations building anew in him. He wasn't healed up all nice and neat, but he was better. With Justice and his newfound family, Paul wouldn't ever slip back into the mess of a man he'd been. He had the strength of love behind him, supporting him, from more people than he had ever imagined he'd have loving him.

With Justice at his side, Paul was only going to keep getting better.

Epilogue

Paul was fidgety, but that was okay. Justice totally understood that. He was nervous about meeting Remus too. There'd been so much talk of the man, Justice was expecting some kind of huge, powerful-looking god.

Instead, an older man with a trimmed white beard and white hair that hung in a braid over one shoulder was led into the cabin by Marybeth.

Remus' eyes twinkled when he looked at Justice. "Not quite what you expected?"

Justice found out he could blush as hard as Paul did. "No, sir." He wasn't going to lie, not when he feared Remus could read his mind.

Paul cleared his throat. "I think Justice meant he thought you'd be more like Cliff. Huge. And scary."

Remus tipped his head in acknowledgement of that. "I am just a simple man. Not too tall, or built like a wall of muscle. Just a man who does the work the Fates set out for him." He gestured at Paul. "Will you let me touch you?"

Paul looked at him like he was off his rocker. "Uh. Maybe? It depends on why."

Justice was wondering the same thing. Remus smiled, and Justice noticed that despite all the white hair, he didn't really look old.

"Because I'd like to say a blessing over you, then over you and your mate both. And I have protection for you each to wear, but I must be the one to put it on you."

Paul jerked back as if the shaman had tried to touch him. "Protection? I thought shifters couldn't get STD's and—"

Remus could blush, too. "Oh, no! No, no, that isn't what I meant at all!"

Laughter came from behind Remus and Justice noticed then that there were other people in their cabin now, too. Paul didn't seem to be aware of the fact that wolf shifters were in the living room, members of Remus' pack.

"I meant these," Remus said, gesturing over his shoulder. "Rolly, bring me the amulets."

"Sure, Dad." A man with dark blond hair strode up behind Remus. He had the same delighted glint in his eyes as his father. "Here you go."

Paul noticed the wolf shifter then. He darted a glance to Rolly, then Remus, then to Marybeth and finally, Justice.

"It's fine," Remus said in a soothing voice. "My son will not harm you, nor will any from my pack. Listen to my heart, Paul."

It should have sounded like a bad romance movie line, but the deeper truth gave the words a weight they would have otherwise lacked. Paul relaxed in minute degrees, until finally, all traces of fear were gone from him.

"You've been hurt, your body, yes, but your heart and soul more so," Remus murmured. "You have a good heart and an old soul. Do not lose faith in yourself, or the goodness of people, human and shifter alike. We are all bound together through the Fates. What shifters and humans haven't learnt, and might never still, is that one cannot exist without the other. Once we were one. Now we are two, yet parts of one whole."

That sounded deeper than Justice was able to process then, but he stored the information away to examine later. Marybeth was nodding, adding quiet hums and encouraging sounds.

And Paul was walking to Remus, his movements easy, trusting. Remus held out his hands and Paul walked right between them. Remus placed one hand on Paul's cheek and the other on his chest.

Justice didn't understand the words that were spoken, but the power emanating from Remus was thick in the air. Paul moaned softly and lowered his head as white light framed his body. Remus' eyes were open, the irises as white as the rest, the pupils white as well. It should have been scary, but Justice wasn't bothered. His mate was getting something from the Fates, something he needed that would help him. It might have only been the ability to forgive himself for ever having got kidnapped, or it might have been a bolster to his strength. Whatever it was, Justice thanked the Fates for giving it.

Then Remus was back to being a normal-looking man, the glow gone as he slipped a leather necklace over Paul's neck. "Justice?" Remus asked.

Justice walked over to stand beside Paul. Remus didn't do the whole glowing, white-eyed thing for him, but that was okay. He did say some kind of strange words before putting a leather necklace with a small pouch around Justice's neck.

"Leave them on as much as you can," Remus told them. "There is power in them." He didn't explain what kind of power, but Justice could feel the pouch warming his skin through his shirt.

"Thank you." He shook Remus' hand.

"It's my pleasure." Remus moved to take a seat at the table. "Now, tell me about this man, Cliff, and what he's been doing."

Justice's phone buzzed. He wanted to ignore it, because it would be rude not to, but Remus canted his head in a slight nod. Justice took the phone when Paul offered it to him, and read the text.

"I think he's crazy, maybe even dangerous, but powerful," Justice said. "He knows you're here."

Remus looked startled by that and he held out his hand for the phone. "May I?"

Justice handed it over.

One left. Will need help with this one, I think. Tell Sabin to be careful. It won't kill him. Remus – we'll meet one day.

About the Author

A native Texan, Bailey spends her days spinning stories around in her head, which has contributed to more than one incident of tripping over her own feet. Evenings are reserved for pounding away at the keyboard, as are early morning hours. Sleep? Doesn't happen much. Writing is too much fun, and there are too many characters bouncing about, tapping on Bailey's brain demanding to be let out.

Caffeine and chocolate are permanent fixtures in Bailey's office and are never far from hand at any given time. Removing either of those necessities from Bailey's presence can result in what is know as A Very, Very Scary Bailey and is not advised under any circumstances.

Bailey Bradford loves to hear from readers. You can find her contact information, website details and author profile page at http://www.totallybound.com.

Totally Bound Publishing

TOTALLY BOUND
Home of Erotic Romance